4

Malcolm, John,
1936-

The wrong
impression

$18.95

DATE			

THE
WRONG
IMPRESSION

•

THE
WRONG
IMPRESSION

JOHN MALCOLM

A Tim Simpson
Mystery

•

Charles Scribner's Sons
New York

Maxwell Macmillan International
New York Oxford Singapore Sydney

Charles Scribner's Sons
Macmillan Publishing Company
866 Third Avenue, New York, NY 10022

Collier Macmillan Canada, Inc.
1200 Eglinton Avenue East, Suite 200
Don Mills, Ontario M3C 3N1

This is a work of fiction. Names, characters, places, and incidents
either are the product of the author's imagination or are used
fictitiously. Any resemblance to actual events or persons, living or
dead, is entirely coincidental.

Library of Congress Cataloging-in-Publication Data

Malcolm, John, 1936–
    The wrong impression/John Malcolm.
    p. cm.
    ISBN 0-684-19252-7
    "A Tim Simpson mystery."
    I. Title.
PR6063.A362W76   1990
823'.914—dc20   90-8500   CIP

10   9   8   7   6   5   4   3   2

Printed in the United States of America

CHAPTER 1

The hospital entrance was tiled in reddish-brown encaustic, rather like the old Underground station at Mornington Crescent. Its swing doors were battered and didn't line up when they came together, leaving an axial gap that irritated the eye like a sprung car bonnet. I shoved one door open and held it for Sue to go through so that together we could savour the full, disinfected, antiseptic aroma of the cluttered entrance hall. Hospitals make me choke with dusty, incipient nausea; this one didn't even look clean. A patchwork of coloured notices, ragged and uneven, covered a motheaten baize board to our right, proclaiming events that were a cross between the coy exclusivity of pregnancy groups and the student ragtime of a technical college.

In front of us was a reception counter with a shabbily-uniformed porter behind it. He was talking partly to a policeman, who leant against the counter on our side, and partly to a cardiganed, middle-aged matron with the bland smooth face and bulging physique that hospital canteen diets impart. All three of them looked directly at us. I looked directly back.

The policeman straightened himself up and eyed me carefully.

'Mr Simpson?'

'Yes. That's me.'

'And, er, Miss Westerman?'

Sue nodded. Down a long corridor ahead of us a nurse stood talking to a porter in that unhurried way that hospital staff usually have. Stretches of boredom punctuated by seconds of sheer terror, that's hospital life; best avoided like the plague.

'Follow me, please.' The policeman paused, as if expecting some response from us, got none, and turned to walk away down the corridor. We followed obediently. He marched briskly through another set of swing doors and

5

turned right down another wide corridor. Against the walls tea-trolleys of empty, dirty plates mingled with tea-trolleys carrying swabs, surgical instruments and disgusting rubber-bulbed coils of unspeakable tubes, like slim, surrealist cobras. We went through a single, spring-loaded door, where another policeman stopped us.

This second policeman was a sergeant, a man larger than the first one and grimmer-looking, more powerful. His uniform strained over his chest. Hanging from the leather strap that the plod encumber their hips with was not a truncheon, but a revolver. He held this lovingly, to stop it from swinging, as he stepped towards us.

'Mr Simpson,' the first bobby announced rather proudly, as though having achieved something concrete. 'With Miss Westerman.'

The sergeant eyed him critically, unimpressed. 'Identification?' he demanded.

The first bobby looked a bit put out. 'Eh?'

'Identification? Have you checked their identification?'

'Oh.' The first bobby became flustered. 'Er, well, surely —' he gestured at us—'from the description alone—'

'It won't be necessary.' The voice that cut in came from a plain-clothes man in a fawn raincoat, quite a clean fawn raincoat as it happened, which covered a dark suit. He was around forty, with neat brown hair and a white shirt collar whose smart effect was somewhat hampered by a brown tie. 'I recognize Mr Simpson. And Miss Westerman.' He held out a hand. 'Hullo. How are you? Remember me? Johnson, Sam Johnson, Chelsea CID? We met a year or two back. Over a Whistler, it was.'

'Oh.' I recognized him quickly. 'Of course. Hello, Sam.'

He shook my hand. 'Hello, Tim. Hello, Miss Westerman. Sorry that the circumstances are so—so unhappy. But now that you're here perhaps . . .' He let his voice tail off.

I became aware that we were in a sort of ante-room smelling of antiseptic where greenish walls had nasty-looking appliances stacked against them. A large, dark-suited johnny was staring at me intently. Next to him was a tired man, three or four years older than me, wearing a long white coat with bits of stethoscope peeping out from one of the side pockets. A doctor, obviously. The large, dark-suited johnny was looking at Sam Johnson rather impatiently.

'Sorry,' Sam then said. 'I haven't introduced. This is Commander Brandon, from Scotland Yard. Commander, may I introduce Mr Tim Simpson and, er, Miss Westerman?'

'Ah.' Brandon's voice was deep and commanding, as befits a Commander. 'Simpson?' He shook my hand, staring straight into my eyes. He was slightly taller than me but a good deal more impressive: about twenty stone to my fifteen. In his youth he must have been quite a packet to handle. His manner was neutral, verging on formal, and not particularly friendly. The dark suit was blue and a pale blue shirt with an impressive neck size faded discreetly behind a dark blue patterned tie. If Sam Johnson aimed to get to Scotland Yard he'd have to reconsider his neckwear; I glanced back at his brown tie and suppressed a wince.

The two uniformed men shuffled their feet and the first one withdrew, chastened presumably, back to his post in the entrance hall. The Commander, somewhat belatedly, turned to give Sue a gallant little bow. 'Miss Westerman. So kind of you to come so quickly. Awful business. Horrible. We can only hope. But it's not for me to say: Dr Redman here will take over at this point. Doctor?'

The doctor was a fairish-haired bloke, thin and tall. He looked weary but gave me an intent stare. 'The patient is in very bad shape.' His voice was quiet, educated, experienced at keeping the calm demeanour. 'Critical, as perhaps you know. We are getting very little response or reaction. This is very distressing for his wife, who is with him now. It's hard to tell if he is reacting properly at all. The damage to the head is of course the serious part of his horrifying multiple injuries. Both legs are broken. He also has a broken arm, several ribs and very severe abrasions.' He paused for a moment. 'There are also two dangerous bullet wounds. It is a miracle that he is alive at all.'

I swallowed. They had told me on the phone that it was

7

bad, that it was not going to be nice, but I wasn't prepared for this. My windpipe began to lock somewhere around the Adam's apple.

Brandon harrumphed and fixed me with an impelling stare once again. 'They shot him twice and subsequently drove over him. He was dragged for a short distance under a vehicle travelling at speed. On the Selhurst Road in South London, the main A213.'

'Who were they?'

Brandon scowled. 'We shall find that out.'

The doctor was still watching me. 'He was brought here from Dulwich, which is near his home. With our special facilities we have done our best and he is protected here, of course, by the Commander's men. The problem is that time is not on our side in this case. Normally it is a great healer. Here, however, we are dealing with possible brain damage. The lack of response is very worrying. The injuries to the head, although serious, do not seem to be so severe as to warrant this condition. His wife has been talking to him but it was at her instigation, quite frankly, that you were sent for. It is not normal and I am not sure if I approve because, quite honestly, he is hovering on a knife edge.' He glanced at Brandon and Johnson. 'These gentlemen consented to what is, I can only say, something of an experiment. I know that they are not motivated by a desire to arouse the patient in order to solve a crime from his evidence, but by entirely humane motives towards their colleague.'

'Absolutely.' Brandon was emphatic. 'The patient comes first. As always. Absolutely.' He glared commandingly at us as though expecting a challenge but got none.

Redman turned back to me. 'I hope that you are not intimidated. You can, after all, only do your best, like us. Are you prepared to go in?'

'Yes.' It came out as a croak in my ears and I swallowed to clear my throat. 'Oh yes.'

The doctor turned and tapped on the door behind him. A rather shapely nursing sister, who looked vaguely familiar, opened it.

'They will enter now,' Redman said.

8

She nodded and opened the door wider.

'Good luck.' Sam Johnson gave me a brief, encouraging smile as I took Sue's arm. 'I'll keep my fingers crossed.'

I smiled back and ushered Sue through the door into the small private ward beyond. Being close behind her, I didn't catch the impact of the situation until she stood aside.

The figure on the high white bed was totally enclosed in plaster and bandages, or so it seemed to me. The legs were strapped and braced. The body was covered by bedclothes but the bandaged and, in one case, splinted arms were out. It was the head that was the stopper, though. It looked like something from Hammer Films. None of the features nor the skull were visible. A pumpkin of swaddled white cloth confronted me. There was a slit somewhere around the eyes and a tube went in, below this slit, to where I assumed the mouth was. Hanging around the whole apparition were further revolting plastic tubes, metal things, meters, gauges. Electronic apparatus bleeped and pumped. There was a smell of ether; the shapely nurse regarded me with what seemed like disapproval. I hate hospitals, as I've said; they make me gag. For a moment I stood still, choking slightly.

Sue let out a small female cry. Then she rushed to a corner of the room. More female cries and sobs came forth as she embraced the tragic, wifely figure that rose unsteadily from a chair. I squeezed one of its arms tenderly and then shoved my hands into my pockets, gritting my teeth. It was time for me to do my stuff. I approached the pumpkin-head resolutely, kneading my hidden fists.

'What ho, Nobby,' I said, bluff as Dover cliffs. 'Who did that? The All Blacks or the Welsh front row?'

There was a penetrating silence. Sue turned and gave me a look of what can only be described as Pained Disapproval. Gillian Roberts, whom she was comforting, tried a wobbly smile and then nodded at me in understanding. The nursing sister gave me a look of obvious contempt. Thin Dr Redman slipped into the room.

The ghastly figure on the bed didn't move but, somehow, perhaps just due to imagination, I sensed a sort of tension in it, a new tension, not easily perceptible but none the less

9

a presence. The bleeping, or was it just my hopefully charged senses, changed tone or frequency or something like that, very marginally. I cleared my throat and took my hands out of my pockets.

'The trouble with you, Nobby,' I said, using the most infuriatingly condescending tone I could muster, 'if you don't mind my saying so, is that you never did learn to side-step properly. I mean, a good centre three-quarter should have learnt how to avoid this type of thing by now. But there you are; you never would listen, would you? Too busy giving other people stern moral lectures to step out of the way of a passing bus. I mean, I don't want to go on or anything like that, you know me, not one to pi-jaw a man in your style, but one of the reasons you didn't get your Blue was because you would go off with not a thought in your ginger topknot, straight for the corner flag without the slightest—'

I stopped. A very small shudder had gone through the white, mummified body. A sound, ghastly by its unintelligibility, gargled from somewhere inside the pumpkin with a horrid rattle of blocked saliva. The nurse shot past me to the side of the bed, seizing pieces of tube. Bleeping and pumping equipment altered its tone and pitch. Dr Redman joined the nurse, scowling blackly, and started twiddling knobs on a control panel. Sue and Gillian, clasped fearfully together, stared at the bed in rigid fascination. Suddenly, there in the swaddled head, deep in the slit towards the top half, there was a gleam, not a bright gleam, not a sparkle, but a faint gleam nevertheless. Then it disappeared, dying like the rattle from the tube entering somewhere round the mouth. The shudder stopped. For a moment the ward was quiet as the other four people turned or stooped in varying intensities and types of emotion.

Nobby Roberts had reacted at last.

CHAPTER 2

Suddenly I was superfluous. Before they shoved me back into the ante-room, everyone trod on my feet. The nurse snapped at me. Gillian Roberts and Sue were allowed to stay, of course, weeping even more copiously than when Nobby Roberts had been entirely comatose.

'—relapse—' I heard Dr Redman saying '—most irregular—I had no idea—jocular nonsense—very, very risky—should have been told the fool might cause a—'

In the ante-room I found myself facing the big rozzer with the revolver. Trolleys came rattling past and I had to jump out of the way. The sergeant looked at me with a relatively favourable expression for a man obviously dedicated to the extermination of anyone even faintly suspicious. Commander Brandon, looking massively pleased with himself, turned to Sam Johnson, who was grinning broadly.

'He's passed out again,' Brandon said, 'but thank God we've got a reaction at last. Redman was afraid he'd never perk up. Glad we agreed to it, though it was a bit tricky, something of a long shot.'

'Thank you, sir.'

Brandon gave me a condescending nod. 'Good show, Simpson. Obliged to you. Bit like a shot of adrenalin.'

'My pleasure.'

'Dangerous, of course, but needs must when the Devil drives.'

'Who did it?'

'Who did what?'

'Who did that to Nobby?'

Brandon checked, straightening himself slightly. 'That is a matter for us to deal with.'

'Arrested them, have you?'

Brandon stiffened. I saw a look of alarm pass over Sam Johnson's decent face. Brandon was congealing as he stood. The sergeant frowned at me.

11

'No,' Brandon said, very formally. 'We have not arrested anybody yet. But we are proceeding with inquiries which I have no doubt will lead to the arrest of Chief Inspector Roberts's attempted murderers. Our investigations will be systematic, vigorous and absolutely ruthless. No one does that to a Chief Inspector of police in this country and gets away with it.'

'Good. We'll be on the same side, then. No one does that to Nobby Roberts, not in any country, and gets away with it. Not while I'm about.'

The sergeant's frown deepened. Brandon licked his lips. 'I appreciate your feelings, Simpson. Appreciate how you must feel. This has been a very distressing experience for you. For all of us. But of course there can be no question of your involvement. None at all. This is a matter for us to deal with. The private citizen has no place, indeed no legal justification, for taking the law into his—or her—own hands. None whatsoever.'

The sergeant nodded smugly. Sam Johnson opened his mouth and then closed it. I rather liked the Sam Johnson I remembered but Brandon was obviously a pompous ass. Into my mind there came an image of Nobby Roberts aged just twenty or so, lean and fast like a hunting dog trimmed in ginger, racing down the wing in some long-forgotten rugby match while we plodders in the scrum shouted our throats hoarse at his back, willing him on. I remembered the swerving clever figure dodging and feinting before plunging brilliantly over the line and the arms thrown skywards in jubilation as we rejoiced. I thought of the more recent staunch friend that he was, how ironically our positions had been reversed; he the tenacious worker with a deep-felt social purpose, me the galloper on the wings of society. Now he was nearly dead, smashed possibly beyond repair. My throat locked again as I thought of that pumpkin-head on the bed nearby.

'Too bad.' My voice had an odd ring to it, a harshness I couldn't control.

Brandon lowered his head slightly so as to fix me with an accusing stare. Antipathy started like static in the air be-

12

tween us, raising bristles like hairs on a dog's back. 'I must warn you, Simpson, against any precipitate action. Warn you very seriously. I allowed you here against my better judgement and even though, as it happens, things have—'

'Against your better judgement?' My voice was working again now, I was cooling, incredulity was coming through.

'Yes. Against my better judgement. In view of your past record.'

'My—my *what?*'

'Past record.' Brandon still held his ground. For a moment we stood, heads lowered, like two rams bracing for a butt. His voice rose. 'There have been too many unfortunate interferences by you in cases involving Chief Inspector Roberts. Far too many. This will not be one of them.'

'Oh, won't it?'

He flushed. 'No, it won't! It certainly won't! Now see here, Simpson. I'm going to be quite specific with you. This is a very serious case, a major murder investigation involving a very senior police officer from Scotland Yard. We can and will not have bungling amateurs tramping around getting in the way. Do I make myself quite clear?'

I gaped at him. It had been quite a while since I'd met a man with as much charm and subtlety as his. Sam Johnson was swallowing nervously. The beefy sergeant looked on with evident enjoyment; the plod love to see someone else getting a ticking-off. Great hackles began to rise on the back of my neck.

'Bungling amateurs, eh?'

'Yes. Bungling amateurs. Stay out of this, Simpson.'

'Good job I didn't stay out of the Brighton affair and Sam here's Whistler business and—'

'That's enough! Quite enough! I remember only too well the cases to which you are alluding! The unnecessary deaths of the woman Gray and the man Benson! Fortunately in other cases Roberts has been able to circumvent your unwarranted intrusion and bring matters to a satisfactory conclusion. If you take so much as one peek into this matter I'll have you arrested for obstruction. Arrested! Is that clear, Simpson?'

I felt myself go hot, then cold. He was a big man, as I've

said, with a considerable presence. The danger with being in such a senior position at Scotland Yard is, I imagine, that you get to thinking that you are God, or at least a lot nearer to the Almighty than your fellow citizens. Brandon must have been a difficult customer to deal with when young but he was well into middle age now, if not past it, and I'd had all I could take of this deprecating surname-stuff. If he just called me *Simpson* in that tone once more I was going to clock him one, Commander or no Commander. I tapped him on the chest with a stiffened forefinger, making his face jerk in surprise. 'Oh, will you, laddie?' I said, using the forefinger to emphasize further points. 'Well, you look here, *Brandon*, I'm a citizen of the Realm, *Brandon*, and when I want to ask you or your minions questions, I'll *bloody well ask them*—'

I stopped. A riot was breaking out. The beefy sergeant had surged forward with a shout of warning, aiming to protect his Commander. Sam Johnson nipped across to get between us. Brandon gave a cry of fury. Four faces, distorted, arrived within inches of each other.

'Gentlemen! Gentlemen, please!' Sam's voice had an urgent, church-interior, desecration-prevention tone to it. 'Really! For Heaven's sake! Think where you are! I must remind you of the circumstances! Please! Gentlemen!'

We checked ourselves guiltily. Sam glared at us both. The sergeant fingered his revolver, eyeing me hopefully.

'Assault!' Brandon gasped incredulously. 'Common assault! The maniac assaulted me, I tell you!'

'Gentlemen, please!' Sam Johnson addressed his Commander frankly, with a considerable absence of respect. 'Sir! Really! Everyone is tense and upset. Mr Simpson is clearly emotionally unbalanced. We must all make allowances. We must all calm down. The Chief Inspector's life hangs in the balance. Think where you are!'

Another guilty silence. The sergeant took his hand regretfully off his revolver. For a second or two we stared at each other in silence. Then a more serious interruption took place, taking us off guard.

The ward door swung open and Dr Redman came through, somewhat short of breath. 'What in hell is going

14

on here? The patient has had a bad enough shock already.'
He gave me a scowl. 'There is to be no further disturbance.
Absolutely none! The danger is acute. I insist that you all
leave, apart from the sergeant. A disgraceful performance!'
His stare remained on me. 'I will not allow disruptive
elements to put my patient at risk.'

'Indeed, Doctor.' Brandon was back in command again.
'I absolutely agree with you. Apart from the sergeant we
shall all leave, as you request. And some of us will not be
coming back.' He stared at me.

'Eh?'

'Not be coming back. To disturb Roberts. To harass him.'

'I beg your pardon?'

Redman nodded vigorously. 'I couldn't agree more, Commander. I shall not allow anyone to see the patient, apart
from his wife, of course. Certainly not Mr Simpson. Not
after this performance.'

Brandon smiled in satisfaction. 'I can guarantee that.'

'You can what?' I couldn't believe my ears.

'I think it would be most unwise to allow a repeat to
occur.' Redman's voice was final, decisive. 'Not at all in the
patient's interest.' His face, turned full to me, was cold.

It was bad luck on him. And Brandon. Statements like
those are nearly always heard by the gods. At that moment
Gillian Roberts came through the ward door supported by
Sue, and saw me. She made a soft, affectionate noise and,
leaving Sue, stepped across to throw her arms around me.

'Oh, Tim! Dear Tim! Thank you so much!'

I held her tight for a moment. The four men in the room
stopped dead in their tracks. Sue looked down, briefly, at
her shoes.

'There, there, Gillian. He'll be all right, you know.'

'Of course he will! Thanks to you! Oh, Tim!'

'Er, well.' I patted her back gently, somewhere between
bra strap and waistband. 'I wouldn't say—'

'You were wonderful! Wonderful! I knew you'd do it.
You've always been his greatest friend. He's always said
that if anything ever happened to him I was to go to you.
You know how much you mean to him; absolutely loyal and

15

dependable. Dear Tim.' She hugged tighter and cried into my shirt front so that I had to pat her again, embarrassing in front of the rozzers but I've always been very fond of Gillian Roberts and was considerably moved myself.

'Oh, Tim! Thank God you could come! Thank God you weren't away somewhere. I didn't think he was ever going to show any—you and he spark each other off so—it was a chance the doctor didn't want to—'

'There, there now, Gilly, it's been a terrible experience, not all over yet by a long chalk—very distressing—we're all a bit distraught—perhaps a large brandy—do us all good—'

'Oh, Tim! So sensible! It could be months before he's anywhere near right and they say he'll never be the same again—God knows—I don't know how he'll—I've dreaded this all my—'

I felt myself go rigid and cold. For a moment it was touch and go. Then I found my bluff-cliffs voice again and did as good an act as I could. 'Not be the same again? Nobby? Good grief, Gilly, a couple of bullets and a broken leg or two won't stop old Nobby from—'

Over her shoulder I caught sight of Redman, hard and cold. Fish have looked at me more approvingly. After they were on the marble slab.

'You will come and see him, won't you? As often as you can?'

'Er, me? Come and see him?'

'Oh, Tim, you must. You will, won't you? Of course you will; it'll make all the difference to him. After me and the children you're—'

'Well, er, of course I'd love to, Gillian, but you see the Commander here and Dr Redman feel that perhaps he ought to, er, well, be kept quiet and calm, so they don't think I should come back and see him. For a while. Er, really.'

Gillian Roberts released me sharply. She stood back and glared with tear-stained eyes at Redman and three suddenly shame-faced rozzers. 'Not see him? Not see him?' She actually stamped her foot. 'I never heard of such a thing!' She shook a finger at them. 'Tim is to see Nobby as often as he likes! Do you hear me? He is practically a brother to us!'

16

Her voice rose hysterically. 'As often as he likes! I am his wife! I—'

Sam Johnson jumped, good fellow that he was, but Sue and I were too quick for him. We gathered Gillian as she began to shake violently and we got either side of her in support as her legs buckled. 'Out,' I said. 'Out we go. You need rest and calm, Gilly.. We'll bring you back when Nobby's had more time. Then we can sort all these things out.' I gave Brandon a winning smile over my shoulder. 'All these things.'

Before anyone else could move we swept Gillian into the disgusting corridor. I caught a glimpse of Redman, still glaring at me. Sue took over as we steered towards the front entrance.

'I'll take her home in a taxi,' she said. 'She's been here all night. It's been dreadful for her; she was desperate when she sent for you. There's nothing more that can be done now, so she must get some rest. Come on, Gillian, you can come back this evening.'

The three reception-figures—porter, policeman and matron—watched in silence as we passed through the badly-fitting doors. I hailed a taxi. Sue and Gillian got in it and I gave the driver his instructions. The cab motored out of the hospital yard and disappeared down the London street, bobbing its black shiny way into the traffic.

The visit was over.

Thus it was that I found myself standing alone on the hospital steps, feeling considerably isolated and somewhat put out.

No, not somewhat put out.

Livid with rage.

CHAPTER 3

Jeremy White sat back in his chair at the top of the table and looked up towards the painting of his ancestor, the founder of White's Bank, hanging over the mantelpiece on his right. His ancestor looked fixedly out of the painting with a distant stare that was directed towards the opposite wall. There was nothing much about the painting that reflected the reality of banking, then or now. The figure was dressed in a blue coat and white silk breeches like a true gentleman, but that particular White founded the Bank's fortunes by trading in rosewood and other exotic timbers from Brazil during the Regency, which was not an occupation favouring white silk breeches at the best of times.

Deprived of any response and still avoiding my eye, Jeremy kept his own gaze similarly focused into the middle distance.

'Parochialism,' he rumbled, for the second time. 'We are being accused of parochialism. Of not taking a—an international—view. Not even a European view, actually.'

I suppressed the urge to smash something. There were three of us sitting at the polished mahogany table in Jeremy's panelled office at the Bank, deep in the City of London. My experience at the hospital, earlier that morning, had left my nerves still a-jangle. This meeting, a regular, long-foreseen meeting of the Bank's Art Investment Fund would, I had hoped, serve as a soothing anodyne, a bland uncontentious review meeting of the sort that simply rubber-stamps the activities carried out since the previous meeting. There was no need for surprises or disputes. The Art Investment Fund, something Jeremy and I had started as a bit of a lark some years before, was intended to trawl in those investors of the Bank's who wanted to put money into art without actually having to buy a Rembrandt themselves. It had done well. The capital appreciation of the paintings, furniture and silver we had acquired was indisputably considerable. Not only that, by taking a thirty per cent interest in Christerby's, the well-known international art auctioneers, we had established the Bank as a leading and respectable figure in the field of art investment. There was no need for barbed remarks, none at all.

The third man at our table, our accountant Geoffrey Price, coughed nervously and looked at me expectantly. Geoffrey is a good bloke, cautious naturally, a great keeper of the score, but not a fervent participator. Prudence is more Geoffrey's style than anything else, as might be expected from a married accountant with four children, a Rover car, and a house in North London. The touchline is the place for Geoffrey, not the pitch.

'These accusations—' I kept my voice calm—'come, I take it, from the other directors here? Other members of the board?'

Jeremy stiffened. Jeremy is a tall man in his mid-forties, still strikingly blond, an Old Etonian with all his family's autocratic and imperious characteristics blended with a large dash of the entrepreneur. Although coming from a minor, cadet branch of the White family, Jeremy had some-how inherited much of the original flair which subsequent generations of Whites, lulled by decades of respectable banking, had lost. It was Jeremy's ambition to power the Bank forward into the modern world, regardless of the semi-comatose family board members who yearned for the quiet life. In this sense the Art Fund was a very minor activity, hardly significant to the main thrust of the Bank's operations, but Jeremy was fond of it. The Jeremys of this world love a gamble, a flutter that stems the flood of boredom, and the Art Fund qualified as that. Jeremy would never lose his interest in it, quite apart from any cultural or intellectual preoccupations.

I had scored a hit. Jeremy's stiffening was accompanied by a tiny nod of the head.

'There have been one or two remarks from other direc-tors,' he conceded. 'Although, as you are aware, I am hardly likely to take much note of what those idiots may say. No, it is from correspondence and, er, well, from correspondence and potential investors that these accusations have come.'

Fiddlesticks. I knew what all this was about. Jeremy was unlikely to take much notice of the multifarious suggestions that came through the post, conveying such requests as those which urged us to invest in postage stamps, tin soldiers, kitchenalia and many other artefacts, all potentially profit-able but outside the scope of art investment as we interpreted

19

it. But other directors needled Jeremy, especially when I well knew that he had a yen to acquire things that would give the Fund prestige. I decided to play the game for a little longer.

'Our specialization, Jeremy,' I said, knowing that it always irritates an opportunist to have basic principles restated, 'has been and is to concentrate on British works of art where we can steal a march on the competition and where such works represent major milestones in the development of art or design here. Any fund, like any collector, must specialize. Otherwise it will not attain any coherency of investment.'

He blinked. 'Coherency of investment? Tim, where on earth do you—'

'Jeremy. Everything we have acquired so far has British associations. But to those who accuse us of parochialism why do you not point out that we have a terra-cotta sculpture of Gwen John by Rodin? And let me remind you that works by Rodin have gone through the roof, especially since this latest book on him came out.'

'But that's just the point, Tim. It's still a sort of—a sort of a British interest rather than a wider one.'

'Jeremy, if we are going to rush out and splash money into the international art market willy-nilly we shall come a tremendous cropper.'

He pursed his lips. 'I did not suggest that we either rushed or splashed! All I am making is the point that perhaps we should consider wider spheres of art investment than those we have currently made.' He peered at me. 'Surely that is a perfectly reasonable suggestion for a member of this meeting to make? Surely?'

I put my hands on the table, cooling the palms on the cold dark polish of the Cuban mahogany. 'All right! All right! I know what this is all about. It was bound to come up again, knowing you. It's about the Impressionists, isn't it?'

Jeremy's eyebrows shot up. Geoffrey Price moved imperceptibly back in his chair and slumped a bit in relief. Jeremy looked from him to me and back again.

20

'The Impressionists have been making tremendous running and the Japanese are snapping them up like a dog with a packet of biscuits. So the pressure is on to snatch one out from under the market's nose. That's what you have been simmering away at, isn't it? Mark you, you've always had a thing about the Impressionists, haven't you? Come on, cough it up.'

He frowned at me. 'You really are the most irritating fellow, Tim. Really you are. If you knew this all along, why didn't you come out with it to start with?'

I grinned at him. Jeremy and I have always understood each other well. The fact that I work for him, am a sort of under-director in a vassal condition to him, doesn't affect our relationship. We've been through too much together.

'I wanted to see how far you'd prevaricate until the truth came out. I knew you wouldn't be able to resist the subject. Who's been needling you? Half the main board?'

He snorted. 'The main board! That pack! You can forget them! Not that they haven't made enough remarks. No, I've been needling myself. We should always have had an Impressionist investment from the start, Tim. It was all so predictable, wasn't it?'

I had to nod in agreement. 'I suppose it was. But we never conceived the Art Fund on such grandiose terms, originally. We saw it as a small, specialized collection that gained ground with subtlety, not a sort of Getty Foundation. We didn't have the money to compete on a grand scale. But art has become such big business and since the Stock Market crash, well—'

'We've got funds pouring in.' Geoffrey made his contribution at last. 'It really is quite amazing. We're cash rich at present.'

To Geoffrey, admirable fellow, it has always been a source of astonishment that anyone would invest in art rather than bricks and mortar, good industrials, banks, or governments of monetarist hue.

'There you are.' Jeremy was quickly assured. 'Cash rich, Tim. Funds pouring in. Time for bold investments, brave moves.'

'Oh, I don't know. It might be argued that the market is at a peak.'

'Never! Remember what Mark Twain said? Buy land, he said, they're just not making it any more. Well, the same applies to Impressionists, Tim.'

'Oh.' I grinned. 'I don't know about that, either.'

'Authenticated paintings, Tim. Properly and expertly authenticated. No fakes, please.'

'Look, Jeremy, someone paid nearly eight million for a van Gogh recently. I know he's a Post-Impressionist and the Impressionists are perhaps more plentiful—relatively speaking—but we could find ourselves locking a very high percentage of the Fund's money into one painting, with all the risk that implies.'

He waved his arm to put my remarks aside. 'We're not talking of eight million. Up to a million was what I was thinking of. That wouldn't unbalance things. Not too much, anyway.'

A look of alarm transformed Geoffrey's face. 'A million pounds? I say, Jeremy, steady on! The Fund only stands at six million or so. Surely we should spread—'

'Spread! Spread! We have spread. All over we have spread!' Jeremy was peremptory. 'It's time to concentrate. A good big solid one, Geoffrey. Something palpable. Something chunky. Mind you, a million is nothing in the art market today. A small slice of a Velazquez, perhaps. Look at that—'

'Jeremy.' I intervened quickly before he got himself carried away. 'If we go competing in the art market for an Impressionist for around a million, we're stepping clean out of our current mould. You have to remember that many of our investors like our Fund because of the way it's structured. Word has got round that we know what we're doing. They like it because it has a British slant. With increasing prosperity, many of our investors are British. Not all of them, but a lot of them.'

'Ha! You see? Parochial! That's what it is! Parochialism all over again. You want a Little British Art Fund for Little British Investors. We're an international merchant bank.

We own a slice of an international art auctioneer. We should use our resources.'

'Resources are not necessarily the same as expertise.'

Silence. He stopped at that. His face set. Geoffrey flashed the whites of his eyes at me. Jeremy is rarely at a loss for a word. Geoffrey and I knew, both of us, that to balk Jeremy completely would do no good, no good at all, to either of us.

'May I suggest a compromise?'

Jeremy scowled. Jeremy regards compromises as a sign of English Civil Service effeteness. Compromises are not for men who shoot pheasants with the one snap shot or else miss completely. And pheasants do not agree to fly at half-speed in order to help out.

'What?'

'I was thinking of the Gwen John thing. The Rodin. A British subject by a French master. We could use the same principle.'

His face lightened, showing interest. 'A British subject? You mean by an Impressionist? But—but who—'

'Pissarro, for one. More important perhaps, Monet.'

'Of course! Monet! My God, why didn't I think of it? Tim, what an excellent fellow you are. We should buy a Monet of a British subject; London, naturally. I absolutely agree.'

'Glad you like the idea.' I could see Geoffrey relaxing perceptibly.

'Have you got one in mind?'

'No, Jeremy, I haven't. And I'm sure it won't be easy to find one, but if, in principle, we are agreed that I should investigate that avenue of investment, I shall be happy to pursue the matter.'

'Tim! Of course we are! Aren't we, Geoffrey?'

'Oh yes. Yes Absolutely.' Geoffrey rolled his eyes at me.

'Splendid! And Sue will be invaluable. She can put in for fees, of course. If the Tate will let her?'

I should explain that my girlfriend Sue Westerman works at the Tate Gallery where she is a Curator, whatever that might be. The Impressionists are a particular interest of hers.

'I'm not sure about fees. But I'll ask her.'

'Excellent! Excellent! That's agreed, then.'

'Providing that you feel that Monet and Pissarro are quite sufficient?'

'Eh?'

'Well, if you are a follower of Wilenski, you believe that Monet, Pissarro and Sisley—who was half-English by the way, so I might include him in my search—were second line. The real masters, according to Wilenski, were Manet, Renoir and Degas. Unfortunately they don't have the British connections we're seeking.'

'Who the hell is Wilenski?'

'Was Wilenski, Jeremy. He wrote one of the standard works on modern French painters. Among much else.'

'To hell with him.'

'Yes, Jeremy.'

'Get on with the Monet and the Pissarro. Forget Wilenski.'

'Very good, Jeremy.'

He grinned at me. 'You are an awful chap, Tim. Really you are. You delight in upsetting our little gatherings. But I'm very pleased at the way your thoughts are going. We must keep up the momentum in the Fund. In the absence of any other business, I'll declare the meeting closed. Geoffrey? Are you lunching today?'

Geoffrey Price shook his head. 'Sorry, Jeremy. Work to do.'

'Worthy fellow. Tim?'

I shook my head, too. 'Sorry, Jeremy. Prior appointment.'

'Oh, Tim, really! You've known very well for weeks that we were meeting today.' He pouted. Jeremy is very fond, now and again, of the generous business lunch, a fading institution which he thinks needs occasional support. 'Surely we could justify it? We haven't lunched together for ages.'

'I know. I'm sorry, Jeremy. But I really can't shake this one off.'

He peered at me suspiciously. 'This terrible business of

Nobby Roberts you told us about this morning—you're not involved in any way, are you?'

'I've been warned off, Jeremy. A big unpleasant Commander called Brandon, from Scotland Yard no less, says he'll slap me in irons if I even so much as inquire.'

'Oh, good. What with the Bank's business and a Monet, we can't have you chasing about after Nobby's attackers like a Boy Scout, can we?'

'No, Jeremy.'

'This man Brandon is absolutely right, you know.'

'Yes, Jeremy.'

'You must stay out of any unpleasantness, Tim. It's essential.'

'Yes, Jeremy.'

He shook his head sadly. 'Why do your assurances only bring a sinking feeling, a sense of utter foreboding, to me?'

'I don't know, I'm sure, Jeremy.'

A look of sharp complicity was shot across at me. Jeremy and his tribe are just that: a tribe. Tribal laws stipulate that if a member of your tribe gets attacked, you always help to clobber the attackers back. His voice, coming across the table, was barely audible but it was quite distinctly clear.

'You will let me know if you need any help, won't you?'

CHAPTER 4

Sam Johnson finished his second whisky and water, put the glass down, looked at me, picked the glass up again, tossed back the drop that had accumulated, put the glass down again and looked at me again.

'I knew I shouldn't have come,' he said.

I picked up his glass and went to the bar to get another whisky for him. All the CID men I've known were drinkers of the hard stuff. We were in a pub south of Trafalgar Square, one that I used to meet Nobby in from time to time, it being convenient for him to march down Victoria Street from Scotland Yard, cut across Parliament Square and come into Whitehall. Nobby liked the pub for its bitter beer and ploughman's lunches, not being a CID man, and I was following the same diet that day. Sam Johnson had eaten a small ham sandwich. It seemed to me that he was under heavy pressure from Brandon and was spending time at Scotland Yard himself, presumably seconded to Brandon in Nobby's absence, but he wasn't very forthcoming about that. I got myself another half of bitter and went back to our table with the drinks. He drank a third of his at one swallow, dislodging his appalling brown tie from inside his jacket.

'I shan't be meeting you again,' he said. 'Not until this is over.'

'Oh.'

I let a silence elapse. Around us people were beginning to finish their lunches, preparing to leave a hard core of drinkers who would stay until the pub closed at three. There was no one I knew in the room, the regulars being mainly civil servants, clerical workers and shopgirls from the Strand. I let my eyes rest on them for a while.

'It was odd, though,' I finally said to him for the second time. 'Old Nobby reacting to me like that. Wasn't it?'

Johnson looked at his glass. 'I don't follow you,' he said.

'Well, think of it: smashed to bits, unconscious. His wife beside him, doubtless talking to him. Nothing. Not a sausage. Nobby dotes on Gillian. Theirs is a very happy marriage, despite his job.'

Johnson shot me a quick disapproving glance and then fingered round his glass. He didn't say anything.

'So why no reaction to compare with mine? Any theories on that?'

'No,' Johnson said.

'Odd, though, wasn't it?'

'I must be going.'

'Competitive, probably, do you think?'

Johnson went still. He took his hand off the glass. 'What do you mean?' he demanded, suspiciously.

I took a sip of bitter. 'Well, think about it. A man's attitude to his wife and family is quite different from his

26

attitude towards his fellow men. Particularly his old college friends. The relationships are made of utterly different elements. At old college reunions there's always that barbed bantering, that jostle for position. Competition. You follow my drift?' I cocked an eye at him.

Johnson's mouth had gone serious. 'No. But go on.'

'Well, imagine it: there you are, smashed up, virtually blotto. You hear your wife's voice. What does that do? Soothes, reassures. You want to reach to her, to tell her you're all right, but you can't move. So you lie doggo, thinking: Thank God, I must be safe so there's no pressure, they've got her to me, if I can just hang on maybe I'll be OK. She's here beside me.'

Johnson shook his head. 'You don't know any of this. Nobby may not have heard anything. This is pure speculation.'

'I got shot once, down in Brighton. Badly. I was with Nobby at the time and he saved my life, but we won't go over all that. I agree I don't know, I'm just guessing, but let's call it informed guessing. So imagine: you're lying there in hospital when in comes a friend, a pal, someone who's part or who's been part of your life. How reassuring: your pals are rallying round.'

I took another sip of bitter.

'Suppose, however, that there'd always been a bit of an element of competition with that pal, something a bit stimulating. What was it that Gillian said? "You spark each other off so," she said. Suppose he's someone who you immediately associate with your own activities in life or some aspect of them, in some way or another? More important, who could be bound up with or play a role in what has just happened to you, or some aspect of it, or could be interested in it? What will your reaction be then?'

'Crazy.' Johnson downed the rest of his glass. 'Absolutely crazy. You've gone off your trolley. I'm off. Before I have to listen to any more of this codswallop.'

'Nobby was on the old Art Fraud Squad for a long time. He and I—'

'Rubbish.' Johnson was vehement, almost as though trying to shake off an image that had come to him.

'Then why? Why the violent reaction? To me in particular?'

He shoved his glass away from him. 'The Art Fraud Squad was disbanded back in 1984. Nobby still did the odd art job now and again because he was experienced, but this was nothing to do with that. Nothing at all. Or to do with you.'

'Oh?'

'Nothing like your Whistler thing, either.'

'No?'

He glared at me. Then he glared round the pub. After a while his gaze softened and he picked up his glass and threw back the drop in the bottom as he had done before.

'Another?'

He shook his head. 'There's work to do. Listen, Tim: I don't want you getting in the way in this affair and I don't want you to waste your time, so take my word for it, will you? Nobby was working on a team—Jesus, if Brandon knew I was telling you this my career would be finished— on a very secret team investigating a big drugs thing. Get it? Drugs. A real nasty hard crowd. Only that type of crowd would do that to a policeman. You have no idea what the drugs scene is like or what it's getting us into. It's not a nice game, it's not pretty and it's international, nothing parochial or particularly British about it. Stay out of this. I know how you feel about Nobby because I'm not exactly detached about what's happened myself. I owe him a lot too. This is nasty. This is no painting-snatcher, no furniture-faker's half-baked scam. This is drugs, big drugs, with big boys, all armed with guns and thumbscrews. I'm sorry to tell you that Brandon was right; there's no room for amateurs in this. You can't get in our way actually, because we're in a field that you have no part in and never will have, not unless you're persuaded to start snorting coke and heroin or whatever. So leave it. Hear me? Leave it. If Nobby pulls through he'll need months of attention, all the support he can get. Think of yourself in that role, nothing else. Friend and counsellor in shock; he'll need several.'

He got up and stood over me for a moment, pulling his fawn raincoat on. As he looked down, his expression eased from the one he'd assumed for his peroration and he started to smile at me over the top of his disgraceful brown tie. I wondered if it was a Christmas present as I spoke up at it.

'What are you smirking at, Sam?'

'You,' he said. 'You haven't changed a bit since I last saw you. You're just the same. I can't think of anyone else who could have poked Brandon on the chest like that and got away with it. Anyone else would be in clink by now.'

'Well, Sam, that was largely thanks to you.'

The smile widened. 'I've been praying for someone to do that to Brandon for years,' he said. Then he went back to seriousness again as he buttoned up the raincoat. 'Nevertheless, it's goodbye, Tim. I meant it. I shan't see you again until this is over. So goodbye.'

I watched him thread his way carefully to the door and open it. Her didn't look back. When the door closed after him I had a moment of sharp evocation as I refocused my eyes. 'If Nobby pulls through,' he'd said. If Nobby pulled through; if, not when. This was a pub Nobby and I used to meet in. I finished my bitter and stared for a while at the remains of the ploughman's lunch scattered greasily over my plate.

I was still seething with rage.

CHAPTER 5

Sue didn't eat much for supper and nor did I. We didn't put the television on. After we'd cleared up she got out a book she said she had to check through for some project or another, an exhibition that the Tate was going to put on. I watched her sit down on the settee, put her feet up, adjust the horn-rimmed spectacles she uses to read with and for defensive armour, and tuck her skirt over her knees. So far it was one of those evenings more observed in the breach than in the whatever. I mean, it wasn't what had been said that was important, it was what hadn't, if you understand me. Sometime soon the storm would break.

Sue Westerman and I had been living together for quite a while. Apart from a gap of a year, when she went to Australia on an exchange which I don't like to talk about, it had been a steady thing. It had made me very happy. We lived in my flat in Onslow Gardens and, as I've said, she worked at the Tate, having been to Oxford and the Courtauld to do her fine art bit. Sue is brown-haired, blue-eyed and reasonably slender but with the right things in the right places. Although slightly feminist and bossy by inclination, she's more than a little bit passionate. I loved Sue; I had asked her to marry me twice or more but she wouldn't, for reasons which are too difficult to deal with now and bound up in her head about whether I'm really reliable, or something like that, and the odd bit of trouble that dogs me, and her career, and mine, and stupid things like those. I was married once before, quite a while ago now, and divorced, so perhaps that was part of it. At least, that was part of the excuse. I find it's no use trying to explain such things; either you're in love with someone or you're not, and I was.

Sue takes her career seriously and she dresses the professional part: tweed or linen suits, neat jackets with blouses, smart shoes. Her life may be art but Sue is no hippy, no Bohemian. She likes to be in control of things. She inherits that side of her character from her father, who was a senior civil servant with the Admiralty down at Bath. He died some years ago and left Sue's mother with a decent pension. Mrs Westerman is a splendid old bird, a tough and peremptory graduate of the old school with whom I'd always got on very well. Sue seems to have inherited a measure of her father's devotion to public service combined with the forcefulness of her mother. They say that apples never fall far from the tree, or some such similar codswallop.

In the flat Sue had hung her paintings close to mine or

around them for contrast. Sue is very keen on the lady artists of England in the twentieth century, people like Laura Knight, Dod Proctor and Elizabeth Stanhope Forbes. My paintings were different, especially the big Clarkson Stanfield marine over the fireplace, a grand nineteenth-century romantic job that Sue never liked. She did admit occasionally to approving of my Gwynne-Jones and the Seago and an etching of Dorelia by Augustus John, but on the whole she was concerned to maintain her own feminine and separate artistic identity. The flat was light and airy. Long windows overlooked the gardens and the Old Brompton Road was not near enough to be too noisy. It's an area of London I feel I belong to and is convenient for work but I might have been more settled if Sue and I had been more permanent, so to speak. She obviously didn't worry about this; although she was in her late twenties she showed no sign of getting broody. My job made me travel and we each maintained a superficial independence, which somehow bothered me, which is why, at the time Nobby got smashed up, we may both have been a bit on edge.

That same evening I was prowling round the flat with something on my mind, a passage I'd read somewhere that kept flickering across the memory of the row with Brandon, Sam Johnson's latest friendly warning, and the sight of that mummified figure on the hospital bed. There is a big bookcase that runs along one wall of the main room and I tracked along it, running my fingers across the spines of the books, trying to recall the piece. Eventually I came across a green cloth book with the black lettering and borderline that characterizes the old Herbert Jenkins imprint. Of course; *Melton Mowbray and Other Memories* by Moreton Frewen. The reminiscences of the old Sublime Failure himself. I found the passage in no time, one that dealt with a late-nineteenth-century hunting and drinking companion of Frewen's called 'Timber' Powell:

His brother had been killed in Somaliland by natives and under conditions involving very base treachery indeed. The news reached Powell in London. 'He was not a

31

brother I was particularly fond of,' he said, 'but it was not to be thought that no effective protest should be made.' Powell took ten thousand sovereigns in gold and started off to darkest Africa, taking with him a brother-in-law called Jenkins. In Cairo they rounded up a dozen cosmopolitan adventurers.

Leaving the coast near Cape Guardafui, Powell reached the district of the crime and he himself shot a chief carrying his brother's field glasses. After a minute search he found the remains of his brother, subsequently confirmed by a dentist's identification of the teeth. He brought the remains back for a Christian burial in England.

Astounding. I blinked at the passage. *He was not a brother I was particularly fond of*. What would Powell have done for a favourite brother? Laid waste the entire Horn of Africa? It was absurd, splendidly absurd, but magnificent, totally egotistical but terrific. *Boy's Own Paper* stuff. It made me feel puny.

Nobby, of course, was not a brother of mine. I have no brothers or sisters. In a way Nobby was more important. There was no one else from my college days who I saw regularly, confided in, got stern moral lectures from, could tell to go and boil his head in that cheerful way you can with blood brothers of that sort. I stopped, holding the book still in my hands.

Blood brothers; there was no one else I owed my life to, no one else who'd drop everything to rescue me. What if I were on that hospital bed, shot and smashed up, knowing little, struggling for life on electric engine-power, pumps and tubes and bleeping dials? Nobby would be out there, stamping an avenging track through debris, danger and obstacle to fix whoever had done it. Nobby would stop at nothing if someone had done that to me. They'd run screaming for their lives.

But Nobby was a policeman.

'What on earth are you muttering about?' Sue closed her book with a snap and got up from the settee in front of the fireplace, under the Clarkson Stanfield, to come round to me. 'What's got into you?'

'Oh, nothing, I—' I let my voice tail off. She knew very well what was wrong with me.

'What's that book?' She grabbed it as I was trying, surreptitiously, to slide it back into the shelf. 'Come on! What is it?'

I frowned. I didn't like the way she'd grabbed the book but somehow something else seemed to be at stake, something that put a nervous tension into both of us.

'Moreton Frewen? Great heavens, Tim, you're not back on to that all over again, are you? I thought we'd finished with that, over and done with—'

The book had opened at the page, the exact page, that I'd been reading. It was uncanny. She stopped as her eye fell on it. I didn't try to prise it away from her, that would have exacerbated her interest and made matters worse. She's a fast reader and as I moved away from the bookcase I almost felt her gaze flicking to my back as she read and looked, read and looked.

When I turned to face her I could see it written all over her face. I can't describe her expression; her voice was low, much lower than usual.

'You're mad, aren't you? Quite mad.'

'Am I?'

Her voice rose. 'That's what the row was all about this morning, in the hospital! You were at it again. Again! You're just like a little boy. Those experienced men were telling you to stay out of things that don't concern you, but no, not you, not Tim Simpson!'

'Sue, I—'

'Now you're reading this! Have you gone completely mad? This is 1988, Tim, not 1888. What are you thinking of? Living in a cowboy film? John Wayne?' She put on a bad imitation of John Wayne's voice. 'A man has to do what a man has to do?'

'Really, Sue, there's no need—'

'Oh yes there is! I know you. I know you so well. I saw it this morning. That look on your face. Someone's bashed

33

your best friend this time so you've got to bash them back. That's it, isn't it? Regardless of the circumstances?'

I licked my lips, which had gone dry. I wanted to embrace her because she looked terrific and I felt sharply how much she meant to me, but she misjudged the facial movement.

'Well, I've said it before, Tim; either I'm in or I'm out. In all these things you get yourself involved with. This time I'm out. If you start to nose into this business of Nobby's, I'm out. It's got nothing to do with art, it's got nothing to do with you and it certainly hasn't got anything to do with me. I'm not going to get myself killed and I'm not going to hang about while you do. Is that clear?'

I put my hands into my pockets. My brain was very alert, almost racing. I'd had nothing to drink that evening, no alcohol, I mean. She seemed so sharply-defined, so well-focused to my eyes that it was as though I was looking at her through clear, brilliant plate glass that somehow magnified and clarified yet distanced her from me. The trouble with this country at present is that it is becoming full of bossy women who think that the only thing a man should do is to work hard, give up smoking, drink and sausages, and generally behave like a neutered cat. In return for which he'll be allowed to have a lemonade and let himself go in coaching the local infants' production of *Babes in the Wood*. Or go jogging, but not late at night and not too fast.

'I haven't said what I'm going to do yet, Sue.'

'No. You don't have to. I can see it on your face, clear as a bell. You're thinking of going off dogging on your own, poking about and dredging up things that are no business of yours. If I let you. Well, I'm not. I'm telling you now: if you start off on one of your escapades over this, I'm leaving. Through that door. I've told you before, either what you do is part of my life or it isn't, in which case I go. This time it isn't, not if you try to do what I think you want to do.'

Behind her the big bookcase was much less clear to my vision, even though I knew the titles of most of the books, reference and fiction, art and business, a blend that I had come to identify with our life together.

'Tim? Are you listening?'

She came back into focus, most clear, most sharp an image, her brown hair waved, her big blue eyes intense, her full mouth set.

'Oh yes, I'm listening.'

'Well?'

'There's no need for this, Sue. No need at all.'

'Don't prevaricate! Either you tell me you'll stop now or I'll leave.' She pointed at the innocent Frewen book. 'This —this incredible madness! You have no idea how dangerous this could be.'

'I think I have.'

'Tim! This is a drugs case! Nobby was on a terribly dangerous case. You didn't know that. Look what they did to him. It wasn't any old robbery or murder; it was to do with drugs.'

'I know. Sam Johnson told me at lunch-time. I suppose Gillian Roberts must have told you?'

Her eyes widened further. 'Sam Johnson? You met Sam Johnson for lunch?' She made it sound like a crime. 'That means you've already started! My God! You've got to stop. Now. Do you hear?'

My hands were in my pockets. I was standing square on to her. 'Sue, I don't think that you should try to dictate to me quite like this. You're upset and it's understandable. But please don't do this.'

'You're crazy! You must stop at once. Or I go. Do you hear? I'm not bluffing, Tim.' She faced me back, square on, just like Brandon, warning me off. It rankled. I had proposed marriage to Sue more than once and she turned me down every time because she wanted to keep her options open. It rankled. She said she wasn't ready. It rankled; I clenched my teeth before speaking. 'In the absence of any formal arrangement between us, I don't think you should try to impose these conditions. You have no basis for it.'

She flushed scarlet. It had sounded incredibly pompous.

'Freedom is freedom, Sue. It works both ways.'

Her mouth opened. For a brief moment she looked straight at me, almost burning her gaze into mine. 'My God,' she said. Then she walked past me across the room

35

to the bedroom door. She went inside and I heard her get a case out of the wardrobe.

I stood stock-still in the living-room listening to her pack. It didn't take a long time. When she came out she had her raincoat on and the suitcase was in her hand.

'Don't go, Sue. Please don't go.'

She paused for a moment in front of the fireplace, under the Clarkson Stanfield. 'I'm going to Gillian Roberts. She needs company at this awful time for her. She didn't ask but I know she'll be glad. No, I'll get a taxi.' She put her face up to look at me. 'At the weekend I'll go to Mother's. I've meant to go for quite a while. When I come back we can make the necessary arrangements.'

'Sue, please.'

'No!'

She walked to the door, opened it and went out without looking round. Then the door closed firmly, without a slam.

I sat down on a nearby chair.

'Shit,' I said, out loud. Then I said a lot more words, out loud, that I'm not going to repeat.

CHAPTER 6

When Charles Massenaux became a director of Christerby's in London he didn't move his office to the marginally more couth rooms higher up and further to the back of the old, cavernous building on Bond Street. He kept the office he'd always had as head of the Impressionist Department in a sort of cubby-hole at the front, upstairs on the first floor. It was one of the few with a window that looked out on to the street. There he was just above the source of all the action below, where porters staggered about grunting as they toted furniture or made ribald remarks as they swung a scarlet nude by Matthew Smith haphazardly on to a stack of canvases.

The dusty little office was lined with shelved catalogues and reference books. Behind a scratched oak desk Charles reclined in a squeaky swivel chair to regard me humorously as I squeezed into the one other chair that the space allowed. Charles preferred to stay in this cupboarded place because he felt that here he was nearer to the reality of things than he would be in the more xenophobic quarters higher up; it made him more accessible. Not that an auctioneer like Charles spent a lot of time in his office, anyway; when not cataloguing piles of paintings he was usually off on his travels, moving smoothly from country house to suburban villa, valuing for probate or gravely giving his expert opinion on a difficult daub whose owners breathlessly awaited a verdict that would either make them rich or drop them back once again to economic obscurity.

Charles Massenaux became a director of Christerby's because we at White's Bank took a thirty per cent interest in the business and we took a thirty per cent interest because Charles Massenaux, a year or two back, had tipped us off that the shares were becoming available. It was a mutually agreeable arrangement. The senior staff and experts had become worried that the firm would fall into foreign owner-ship and since we, as perpetrators of the Art Fund, were both a bank and an art investor, Charles had come to me and Jeremy as friendly predators. There was no real nepotism in ensuring Charles's elevation to the board of Christerby's once we had secured the shares; he was highly professional and a widely acknowledged expert in his field.

'How pleasant—' his tone was mocking—'to be honoured with a visit from one of our directors. The man himself. Today is not one for a board meeting by any chance? Or are you, as a non-executive member, simply checking that we are keeping good office hours? Doing a fair hand's turn for our little crust?'

Charles is a smooth cove. There's no other way to describe him. He wears dark pinstriped suits rather like me, has highly-polished black shoes, ditto, and tends towards white, blue, or striped shirts with sober ties, also ditto. In short, his appearance is more like that of a banker or an undertaker than a fine art expert, but that's the London trade for you. They all dress that way because their clients like to deal with professionals, nothing too flash, good sober-looking men who might just have served in a decent foot regiment but not a fashionable one and certainly not in the cavalry. Charles's face is long and pale and his dark hair waves unostentatiously over his aristocratic head. He tamped the hair down now with a characteristically smooth stroke of his well-kept hand as he watched me try to cross one leg over the other in the confined space.

'How nice to see you, too, Charles,' I grunted, 'and not at a boring meeting, either. You look well. News of your fame has filtered even as far as the City, where the frenzy of exchange normally allows little time for art news to permeate.'

'How kind. How kind. We have, as it happens, been doing rather well.'

'Very well. Very well indeed.'

'Turnover has increased,' he agreed modestly. 'So have profits.'

'Mainly due to your Impressionist sales.'

'Mainly due to our Impressionist sales,' he agreed again, just as modestly, 'but other departments have been doing well, too.'

'Furniture, for instance.'

'Furniture, I agree. Especially Georgian furniture. Mahogany, you know.'

'Indeed. Indeed I do. And Old Masters.'

'Old Masters, to be sure, have done well.'

'But silver has languished.'

'Silver, indeed, has—listen here, Tim, are we going to go on cooing at each other like this or are you going to come to the point? I haven't got all day to spend, you know, quacking platitudes at you of all people.'

'How uncouth! Does this establishment run to coffee or do I have to send out for it?'

He frowned. 'This is not a coffee-house. These are sale rooms. However, for a non-executive director I suppose an exception could be made.' He picked up a telephone and issued instructions. 'I must say that you do look a little— forgive me—distrait? In need of coffee. As though sleep had come not to the troubled breast, or words of that sort?'

'Sleep does not usually come to breasts that are troubled, Charles, but let's not go into all that. Fact is, I'm after a Monet, a Pissarro, and possibly a Sisley. In that order.'

For a moment I thought he was going to lose his composure. Fortunately for him a rather superior girl came in carrying a tray containing two coffees, milk, and sugar. I had no doubt, knowing London auction rooms, that this up-market female coffee-carrier probably had first class honours at Oxford, had studied in Florence, Venice, Rome and Geneva, and that her daddy had a thousand acres near Newbury, but that's the way it goes in those establishments. Five thousand a year and the coffee to make just for the privilege of spending time on the premises and being worked to death on cataloguing.

He saw me watch her go out and grinned knowingly. 'Not bad, eh? She knows more about Titian and Botticelli than anyone here and most at the National.'

'The coffee's not bad, either,' I said, giving it a sip. It was true that I needed it. The previous night had been somewhat sleepless, as Charles had guessed.

He grinned again and them composed himself. 'I take it that these canvases are for the Art Fund, not for your private collection?'

I gave him a reproachful glance. Contrary to popular belief, auctioneer-experts like Charles are not luxuriously paid, not compared with lower-level City share salesmen. Charles was always harassed about his children's school fees and he had a habit of needling me about merchant bank salaries. I have to admit that I made a lot more than Charles and didn't deserve it, but that's the way the world is.

'I'm afraid I'm not in the Impressionist bracket, Charles,' I said. 'The plan is to buy them for the Art Fund, yes.'

'Ah. And why, if I may ask, the choice of those particular three?'

'Good question. A question I would have expected of you. Because of their English work. Or rather, I should qualify that, their painting in England. We are an English—or rather British—Fund. We would like to buy Impressionists but with an English slant to them, you see.'

'Ah.' He made a dismissive gesture. 'What you mean is that you don't want any old rubbish like Manet or Renoir, what you want is to buy something like, say, Monet's 1870 painting of the Houses of Parliament, currently in the National Gallery? Or the Pissarro of Charing Cross?'

'Precisely, Charles. Precisely. You have grasped the situation with characteristic acumen.'

He picked up a catalogue and began to whiffle through it, adopting a higher-pitched throwaway tone of voice. 'No problem, I'm sure. Let me see, we have two or three coming up at our next regular sale, or perhaps more, but if you would care to wait for the late autumn, higher-quality sales, we should perhaps be able to offer several better—'

'Charles!'

He put the catalogue down. 'My dear Tim. My very dear Tim. Have you got the faintest idea what you're asking for?'

'Not easy, I realize.'

'Not easy! Not easy! I love the understatement. Monet, as I am sure Sue will have told you, was in England during the Franco-Prussian War, when he and Pissarro took refuge here. He came back in about 1900 and painted some more. Pissarro has greater associations with England and was here more often, especially since his son Lucien settled here and then there was Orovida and so on, but I'm sure that Sue will have briefed you on all this.'

'Ah. Well, er, I haven't had much time to—'

This was embarrassing. I'd had rows with Sue before but never one like the previous night's. Thoughts of Nobby and that situation had put my meeting with Jeremy clean out of my head. It was only after Sue had departed that I had remembered with bitter suddenness that I hadn't asked her for the information I needed.

'My dear Tim, your charming and delightful lady, quite apart from being an ornament to the Tate Gallery, is a first-rate expert on the French Impressionists, as I am sure you are aware. There are several aspects on which I defer only to her. Phone her up to ask for her opinion and so on.

40

I take it that you have come here to pump me for general information only in so far as the crass commercial aspects are concerned? About how much one would have to pay and so on?'

'Um, yes, but I did need a bit more.'

He frowned. 'I'm sure I can't add much to what Sue could tell you in an academic or historical sense, or at least on the sources to go to.'

'Look, Charles, the fact is that Sue's gone away for a bit to visit her mother.'

'Surely it will wait till she gets back? You don't actually have to buy the painting this afternoon, do you?'

'It may be a bit of time. A bit of time before she's back.'

He put down his coffee cup, which he had been raising from its saucer, very suddenly. 'Good God! Tim? You don't mean she's—she's actually Gone Home to Mother, do you?'

'Er, well, yes.'

'With capitals?'

'With capitals.'

'Christ!' This time he did lose his composure. 'Bloody hell! What on earth happened? Or rather, should I ask who the other woman is?'

I compressed my brows. 'There is no other woman, Charles. Or other man, to my knowledge. We had a row. A rather major row.'

'Good grief. Dear me. Would you like some more coffee?'

'Yes, please.'

'Brandy?'

'No, thank you.'

He rang again. 'This is a shock. Quite a shock.'

'Indeed.'

Fresh coffee came. I drank most of it. Charles regarded me steadily. 'I'm sorry,' he said finally. 'Very sorry. Anything I can er—can—'

'No, thanks. It will have to work itself out.'

'Was it, er, was it a major—um—matter that—'

'It was about Nobby Roberts.'

'Oh dear. I was very sorry to hear about Nobby. What's the situation?'

41

'In the balance.'

'Oh dear.' There was a tactful silence. After a while he looked at me again. When in doubt, especially in emotional matters, an Englishman will change the subject. 'Look, Tim, to revert to your question. The paintings that Monet and Pissarro did in England are pretty well documented as far as it is possible to document any paintings by any artist. I should forget Sisley, if I were you. His father was English, a silk merchant in Paris who lost his money dealing with South America, and Sisley finished up rather miserably in the end. I don't know of any English subject he ever did. It's Monet's garden paintings at Giverny that have had all the publicity lately—they say the next one to come up will go for over three million—but if one of his earlier English scenes came up it would be hellishly expensive too, I can tell you. Pissarro would be less; you might do better there; you'll still pay a lot. It's not as though Penge Station is going to come up again, you know. But it's a line worth pursuing, if you'll forgive the pun.'

'Thanks. You don't know of anything coming up in the rooms?'

He shook his head. 'No. It's amazing what has happened. I mean, Monet's *Terrasse à Sainte Adresse* was sold twenty years ago by Christie's for £560,000. That was a world record for a Monet then. One of his most important paintings. It would probably be more than ten times that now, there's so much money chasing the major Impressionists. No, Pissarro might be a better bet for you.'

'You don't know if—'

He shook his head. 'No, I don't.'

'What about the galleries?'

He hesitated. A reluctant look came into his face. He gave me a rather quizzical look. 'There is one. But you won't like it. Won't like it at all.'

'Why not? Which one is it?'

'Not one of your favourites.'

'Oh no! Not Morris Goldsworth?'

He nodded sadly. 'I'm afraid so. Apart from the rooms and the really expensive galleries like Kennard & Crowe,

42

or some other Bond Street mob, the gallery that has pretty good contacts and a specialization in that type of painting—Pissarro, I mean—must be Morris Goldsworth's. Knowing your feelings for each other, it's not a promising start. But I give it to you as a thought, if you're determined to go this route.'

'Jeremy's very keen to get in. Especially since the Japanese are buying like mad.'

'Ah. I might have guessed.'

'There's pressure from Jeremy.'

'I can imagine.'

I got up. 'Thanks a lot, Charles. As usual. When I've a bit of time we must lunch together.'

'That would be nice.' He looked up at me. 'Tim, er, if you'll forgive my asking, this row with Sue: you said it was to do with Nobby Roberts?'

'Yes.'

'Tim, it wasn't—because—you weren't aiming to do anything about what happened to him, were you? Yourself, I mean?'

I didn't reply.

'Were you?'

I opened the door. 'Thanks a lot, Charles. See you soon.'

He shook his head. As I closed the door I heard his voice, reproachful and sad, softly admonishing.

'Oh, *Tim*.'

CHAPTER 7

In one day the hospital entrance hadn't changed at all. No new doors, no smarter notices on the board. The same uniformed policeman was leaning against the same reception counter talking to the same tatty porter in the same scruffy uniform. The fat matron was sitting at a typewriter chewing sticky fruit pastilles, the open packet in front of her. She looked up as I entered.

The policeman faced me with incredulity. The porter

43

glanced from him to me and back again, and then to the matron.

'Good afternoon,' I said cheerfully.

'Mr Simpson?' The bobby sounded as though he couldn't believe his own ears.

'Correct. To see Chief Inspector Roberts.'

He gaped. The matron had stopped clacking the typewriter and was regarding me, her mouth slightly open, poised in the middle of a chew.

'Matron,' I said to her in respectful acknowledgement.

'Not a hope,' the policeman said.

'I beg your pardon?'

'Not a hope. Of seeing Chief Inspector Roberts.'

'Why not?'

'The Chief-Inspector-is-allowed-no-visitors,' the policeman recited, getting it off pat. 'None at all.'

'Oh. How is he?'

'No change, sir.' The bobby's voice returned to normal and I saw him now as rather young and gangly and earnest, with a red, well-scrubbed face and a white line of skin round the edge of his short hair where it had been cut and shaved close. 'No change from yesterday. The Chief Inspector is holding his own, but—'

'Conscious?'

'No, sir.'

'And I can't see him?'

The young bobby's face changed. 'Good God, no. It'd be more than—especially not you. I must say I'm a bit surprised that you—'

'Why not?'

'Why not? After your donnybrook with Commander Brandon? Let alone what Dr Redman says. Didn't they tell you? At the time?'

'Tell me what?'

The well-scrubbed face took on a slightly awed but humorous expression.

'Here—did you really duff up the Commander?'

'What?'

'Sergeant Birtwhistle says that he had to rescue the

44

Commander from you. Duffing him up good and proper, he says you were.'

'Nonsense. Merely making a few discussion points, as a free subject of the Realm, with the aid of a forefinger.'

'Cor. Well I can tell you, you're on the black list. Good and proper. I mean, no one except official parties and the Chief Inspector's wife are allowed access to him. But especially not you.'

'Contrary to his wife's express wishes?'

'Sorry. Not a hope.'

'No way I can get in touch?'

'Sorry.' He stood carefully in front of me, blocking the way.

At that moment the corridor door opened and a nursing sister, neat and trim and experienced, trod across to dump a sheaf of papers into the matron's in-tray. I recognized her at once; it was the rather shapely nurse who had been tending to Nobby the day before. I jumped across to intercept her, forestalling the bobby's involuntary blocking move.

'Sister?'

She was in uniform of course, packaged in stripes and a white apron-like thing on her chest with a sort of bib, and a starched white hat and dark stockings and sensibly flat shoes. Her hair, I now noticed, was light brown, tending towards blonde, tucked neatly about her head and framing a face that was fair, with blue eyes. The shoes made her look a bit shorter than I had remembered her but she was still very feminine despite the desperate disguise that some hospitals make nurses wear. She had stopped, and was looking at me without recognition or friendship. Her face set into an official expression conveying semi-hostility. As her jaw stiffened and her back went vertical in an attempt to look down her nose at me I remembered her contemptuous glances of the day before. Then a blessed flood of memory came to save my day.

'Theaker, isn't it? Katie Theaker?'

Her gaze flickered. The policeman took an interested stare at us.

45

'I knew you as Nurse Theaker, didn't I? Katie Theaker? We used to pull your leg and say you'd be Sister Kate one day and be able to shimmy with the best of them.'

Down the corridor, out of the corner of my eye, I suddenly saw Dr Redman come out of a ward somewhere, wearing his long white coat. He didn't see me, fortunately, because he was talking rather animatedly to another nurse, one perhaps a bit younger than the one in front of me.

She hadn't seen Redman. My nursing sister's look at me was flat and unwelcoming. Not a flicker of pleasantry crossed her face.

'I remember you,' she said, without expression. 'But I'm afraid I'm rather busy. I'm on duty in Chief Inspector Roberts's ward and he mustn't be left. I just popped out to give matron these papers.'

'Oh.'

She now saw Redman, I noticed it; her look had gone from me to a point up the corridor. Redman had his hand on the other nurse's shoulder.

'You used to go out with a chap who played for Tommy's —St Thomas's Hospital—called Bungo Saunders. Second row man. I remember you clearly. We met a few times at the usual thrash after their match with us.'

'Yes.' Her eyes weren't looking at me. Redman was a tall thin man, as I've said, and he stooped now to put his ear close to the nurse's mouth.

'Often wondered what happened to old Bungo,' I said, as amiably as I could. 'Jolly hospitable bloke, as I recall.'

'I married him,' she replied absently. Her blue eyes had gone steely hard and distant, focusing away up the corridor. A gust of laughter came from Redman and the nurse.

'Did you really? Good gracious, how splendid. How is old Bungo?'

The eyes traversed like a pair of blued barrels on a naval double gun-turret and fixed rigidly on mine.

'I divorced the great rugby-playing, beer-swilling oaf two years ago,' she said.

Silence, except for a faint gasp of delight from the fat matron. There's not much you can do when hit in the solar plexus. Not much except gape a bit and gasp for air. I took in, rather as though it were a frozen tableau, our group in the entrance to the hospital. The young policeman was upright, all attention, but immobile. The porter was standing with his eyes fixed on me in petrified fascination, smirking slightly. The fat delighted matron had closed her mouth and was crouched behind her motionless typewriter with her beady eyes fixed on me in triumph. Redman now put his arm round the nurse in a rather unprofessionally friendly movement.

'In that case,' I said, finding my voice at last and thinking there was nothing really to lose any more now, 'perhaps we could have a drink together when you come off duty?'

She had turned to watch Redman and the nurse but her gaze flicked back to me. 'I beg your pardon?' she asked, as though she hadn't heard me correctly.

'A drink. I wondered whether I could buy you a drink when you come off duty?'

The policeman's jaw dropped about an inch. The matron's beady eyes went completely round. Sister Katie Theaker stared at me uncomprehendingly. She seemed to be having difficulty understanding me.

'Are you—are you—asking *me* out for a drink?'

I nodded carefully. 'I am. Indeed I am. Such things have been known, you know. People do, I am told, stop and have a drink when they finish work for the day. It can happen, in our society, and even in Russia. Even before glasnost and perestroika.'

She still stared at me. 'This evening?' Disbelief made her voice high.

'This evening. There used to be a little pub down the road, I recall, known as the Beetle and Wedge or something like that, where tired medical men—and women—used to go at the end of their wearing stints of duty. What about there?'

Her eyes were widening. 'It hasn't been called the Beetle and Wedge for nearly ten years. It's called The Houseman now.'

'The Houseman? Good grief, whatever next? How absolutely appalling. Perhaps you would prefer somewhere else?'

Up the corridor Redman gave the nurse's arm a distinctly intimate squeeze and separated from her, heading away from us without looking round. I tried one last, desperate card.

'They won't let me see Nobby, d'you see,' I said to her face as it watched Redman disappear and the nurse trip lightly back to her ward. 'They won't let me near him. I need some help. The doctor seems to be particularly biased against it. I think he's taken a dislike to me.'

Redman vanished. The nurse capered through her ward door with a marked swing of the hip. An expression compressed Sister Theaker's face as she stared at the now-empty corridor. Her eyes came back to mine, very determined.

'The Houseman will do,' she said. 'I get off at seven o'clock. I'll see you there at half past.'

'Oh. Great. That's splendid. The Houseman at half past seven, then.'

'Good.' She turned to go and then stopped. Her face set in a more official, more formal mode. Her back stiffened. 'Don't get the wrong impression,' she said. 'I don't make a habit out of this sort of thing.' Then she was gone, disappearing up the corridor to the door that led off towards Nobby's ward.

The entrance tableau had crumpled considerably. I turned to the three of them and nodded brightly.

'Constable,' I said. 'Porter. Matron. A very good afternoon to you all. Until the next time, perhaps?'

The policeman beat me to the exit. He stuffed his helmet under his arm in an official, doffing movement and stood to attention as he held one of the ill-fitting doors open for me. 'Good afternoon to you,' he said, with a grin and an expression of gratifying respect that somehow also included a broad wink. 'Mr Simpson. Sir.'

CHAPTER 8

'We did have one, sir.' The soft-suited young impresario at Kennard & Crowe sounded genuinely regretful. 'But I'm afraid that it was sold a while ago. Very quickly.' He smiled at me in happy confidence. 'I'm afraid that the Impressionists are like that now, you know. Anything good goes very quickly.' He gave a gesture at the big black album I was standing over. 'There are many other interesting items we can show you, if you like . . .' An eyebrow was cocked at me inquiringly.

I frowned irritably at the clear plastic folders contained within the album. I wasn't after a Vlaminck. I didn't want a Mondrian or a Modigliani or a Braque, fine though they might be. I wanted a Pissarro, and a Pissarro of London at that. Kennard & Crowe, until recently, had had one.

'Even the photograph has gone,' I objected. 'I can't even see what it was like, to follow it up and find out if the buyer might be interested in a deal on it, perhaps.'

This was true. The clear plastic folder in which the photograph would normally be contained was empty. Only the entry in the index at the back of the album, which I had combed perhaps a bit more assiduously than the usual customer of Kennard & Crowe's, remained. View in Lower Norwood, by Camille Pissarro, 1871, it said, catalogue no. 36. Tactfully, there was no price. When you turned to no. 36 though, there was nothing, a blank space. This was irritating.

The young impresario shook his head and smiled slightly at the idea that anyone who had paid the price that Kennard & Crowe charged for a painting could possibly trade it on to anyone but an economic lunatic. He was a tall young man with thinning fair hair and his suit was evidently woollen, of a sort of soft fibrous quality that was probably Italian and was certainly very expensive; not a suit to wear in the rain.

'Not a hope, sir,' he said, taking an unknowing cue from the young constable at the hospital. 'This was a private collector, most specifically. In normal circumstances we might approach the buyer concerned on your behalf to see if a re-sale could be considered.' He sounded like an estate agent; well, it's a similar way of life, I suppose. 'But this, er, this client was adamant. It was for a collection which he is building up.' He leaned forward confidentially. 'New City money, you know. Actually, we were very pleased because it was a UK buyer—nice to know that some yuppies are using their money well—and the painting would stay in this country.'

'So off it went.'

'Indeed it did.'

'And no export problems to delay it.'

'Oh no. No export problem, because it will stay here. Actually, there isn't usually too much problem in exporting such paintings, although I must say something special with UK interest, like that, can be a bit tricky.'

'I see. Damn.' I refrained from asking him how anyone was to know if the buyer simply put the painting in the back of his car and drove to Paris with it, because although that would technically be illegal, my experience of driving to the Continent is that no one looks into a car leaving, or arriving from, Britain. However, that would merely have prolonged a conversation I was already starting to find tedious as well as frustrating. I didn't like the young impresario or his gallery. I was, actually, indulging in what is known as a displacement activity. Kennard & Crowe were in central Bond Street—in fact I was almost opposite Charles Massenaux's eyrie at Christerby's—but they were not a place I would normally look in to for paintings for the Fund. They were horribly expensive, with a clientele that was too lazy and too wealthy to attend auction rooms. I was there because I hadn't yet summoned up the will to go and enter Morris Goldsworth's. I was there because, walking up the street to get to Goldsworth's, I had passed their window and plunged in, knowing that they dealt in modern French painters in a horribly parvenu sort of way and that there

50

might be something of interest to see. There wasn't, but my heart had leapt while I was paging through the standard album or catalogue of photographs that all galleries proudly leave out for prospective clients to page through. I had thought that I might be on to a Pissarro, a Pissarro of London, but I wasn't.

'It must have been quite rare,' I said resentfully.

'Oh yes. Quite rare. It is generally held that Pissarro only painted a very limited number of canvases as a result of his stay in 1870 and 1871, but of course that is open to debate.'

'Is it?'

The young impresario smiled indulgently. 'One of the documented London paintings—*The Church on Westow Hill in Snow*—has a complete set of preparatory drawings in existence for it. They show how rigorously he worked on the structure of the composition. There is no reason why he should have limited himself to only one or even a set number of finished works of these London oils. Many artists have produced more than one final version of an oil painting. He lost a lot of paintings destroyed by the Prussians in his home in France—they used it as an abattoir, and his paintings as paving to soak up the blood—so there's no reason why he might not have produced a few more when he got back, to make up.'

'I see.' The story inclined me leave. 'I suppose not.'

'If there's anything else I can do—'

'No. No, thanks.'

He smiled again. I stamped out of the gallery and closed the door as I went on to the pavement of Bond Street. I knew I shouldn't have entered Kennard & Crowe. They were the sort of smoothies who always set my teeth on edge. Rumour had it that they had unlimited funds supplied by some sort of syndicate. Not the sort for the Bank's Art Fund to compete with; high-fliers, big-time boys with more money than sense, laying on the prices with a trowel.

I strolled towards the Piccadilly end of Bond Street, heading for Morris Goldsworth's. The aroma of perfume from the traditional soap and perfume companies which jostle each other there wafted to my nostrils as I looked at the paintings and carpets that presented themselves along the way. Agnews had an exhibition on—I think it was Bernard Dunstan—and I remembered that when time permitted I should go over a street and see the Bill Jacklins at the Marlborough. There's never enough time to keep up with all the art that's about. Crossing the pavemented divide from the old street to the new, I remembered, too, that there was a Mary Godwin at the Fine Art Society I had promised to see, but, bringing back memories as it would, it was probably best left undisturbed by me just now. I needed my strength for Morris Goldsworth. Contrary to popular opinion, from Commander Brandon at one extreme to Sue Westerman at the other, I do not go out of my way to invite unnecessary conflict; it does enough finding of me by itself. Morris was not enamoured of my forays into what he regarded as his territory; hence my dawdling along the way.

Outside the glass-panelled door to his gallery, I paused. Although reflections half-obscured it, and there was a poster for some exhibition or another pasted to the panel, the peace within was evident. A girl sat at a desk at the far end of the long cool room that served as the gallery. Cheerful paintings hung on the walls, carefully lit by spots on ceiling rails and in corner clutches. There was no one in, no one looking at the stock at all. The girl was reading a magazine. With an effort that felt as though something physical was resisting it, I turned the door handle and went in.

The girl looked up, smiled briefly and looked back at her magazine. I took stock of the stock, so to speak. Morris Goldsworth was heavily into what you might call the plein-air tradition. Cheerful country scenes of the turn of the century mingled with bright marines, harbour and coastal scenes of the West Country and Brittany. Terrick Williams nestled among minor Newlyn School artists. The odd Scotsman like Sir David Murray put breezy landscape alongside bovine meadows from English Post-post-Impressionists. It was safe stuff, unchallenging and idyllic, carefully cheered up by judicious relining that trimmed boring passages and subtly restored so that skies were a little bluer, the sun a little brighter, the grass a little greener and the girls a little prettier than perhaps the original artists intended. Don't get the idea that I blamed Morris for this; selling paintings is a deadly psychological occupation and Morris knew what his customers wanted, what they were prepared to accept. They didn't want angst, they didn't want misery, they didn't want a challenge or something that their friends would laugh at, they wanted well-documented artists, artists who were 'in the book', the reference books that meant, artists who had exhibited at the Royal Academy or some recognized venue, who had a safe track record, who would maintain value. The fact that Morris Goldsworth, like all sellers of art and antiques, was selling illusions, self-assuring mirages that existed only in the minds of the purchasers, was something none of his customers would have liked to have explained to them. That the objects we surround ourselves with are the reflection of an indulgent self-image is not the business of a dealer to explain; like a Ferrari salesman, he is there to flatter the prospect's idea of himself and to moisten his palate by suitable references to the prospect's excellence of taste and bravura in self-display.

A door opened at the end of the gallery and a large man in a dark suit stepped through. Morris Goldsworth is tall and hefty, running to a waistline in the upper forty inches. His tie sloped down his chest like a ladder on a church roof. He wears very thick tortoiseshell spectacles that make his eyes seem frozen into his head; it is difficult to follow their expression usually, but now, as he saw me, the emotions crossing his face were evident. A dark scowl brought his black eyebrows down to meet the tortoiseshell frames at the top.

'Simpson! What the hell are you doing in here?'

'Hello, Morris. How are you?'

He took two quick strides towards me. 'What do you want?'

'I—'

Before I could answer, his voice bellowed, 'I've told you I don't want you sneaking in here, snooping about! Get out!'

'Really, Morris, really! Calm down! I've come to see you on business. And on another matter.'

'I don't need White's Art Fund to—' A look of deep suspicion crossed his face. 'What other matter?'

I looked past him to the empty room, only inhabited by the girl, who was watching in riveted fascination. 'Where's your minder?'

Morris Goldsworth was in the habit of employing a male assistant, usually either a large young man of ex-public school origins whose parents felt that the fine art trade might be a suitable occupation for an offspring who failed his exams with depressing regularity, or else a working-class Londoner like Morris himself, useful physically and with perhaps the nous to become a dealer of sharp, rat-like cunning. Unfortunately most of the bright young dealers without personal money are to be found in the City these days, wallowing in stocks and bonds. Morris's assistants were prone to a rapid turnover and few of them were any good with their fists; they just looked threatening, which is enough to scare most people.

'He's moved on to—Here! I don't need a minder to take care of you! I'll call the police!'

'Oh dear, Morris, dear, dear. This will never do. I am here on genuine business.'

'What kind of business?'

I glanced at the girl. 'Is there somewhere we could talk?'

He glared at me. 'You can see my stock. If you want to buy anything, the price lists are on the table by Cathy's desk.'

'Morris.' I adopted as mollifying a tone as I could muster. 'I know that you and I have clashed in the rooms and that you don't like our Art Fund. Nevertheless, we are here to stay and we can't buy all the things we would like to buy at auction exclusively because they don't all come up at auction. We do buy from dealers as well. We have bought from dealers as well. You surely know that.'

He blinked. The glasses magnified the action considerably, making it look as though a shutter had briefly dropped across his eyes. I waited until he'd focused on me again before speaking.

'It concerns the Impressionists.'

He blinked again. 'What—the French Impressionists?' Disbelief was coming into his voice and disinterest with it.

'Yes. But I'm talking of their painting in England. Like, say, Pissarro?'

His eyes now widened instead of drooping and he bent his head forward as though to hear me properly.

'Pissarro?'

'Yes.'

'His painting in England?'

'Yes.'

He gave a brief glance round, then looked back at me cautiously. For a moment he seemed irresolute. Then he half-turned away from me, speaking over his shoulder. 'You'd best come into my office. It's as dead as Cork Street in here. Moribund. Terrible.'

'Thank you, Morris.'

I followed him respectfully through the empty gallery, smiling inwardly at his reference to nearby Cork Street, where celebrated contemporary art galleries put up today's painters in an atmosphere of almost total immobility. At the back of the long room we went through into a surprisingly light but small office, where there was a pedestal desk up against one wall and two spare chairs round a coffee table. On other walls were shelves with files and office paraphernalia or, opposite, a painting by Harold Harvey hanging on its own. Morris gestured to a chair and I sat down on it.

'Like a cuppa tea?'

'Yes, thank you, Morris.'

'Or do you lot go in for something stronger?'

'Tea will be fine, thanks. No sugar.'

He put his head round the door. 'Get us two teas, Cathy, there's a good girl. One without sugar. The usual for me.' Then he sat down on the other spare chair and settled himself into it uncomfortably. His pupils widened through the thick lenses as the tortoiseshell glasses ranged themselves on me.

'I'm a Chelsea boy, myself,' he said, with apparent irrelevance.

'I know, Morris. I remember, from that Whistler business.'

He frowned. 'That was a bad business. And you wound up taking the goods.' A movement made the eyes jerk away behind the lenses.

'Er, yes, we did.'

He crossed his big legs, making the dark material of his trousers strain across the knees. 'At least you kept the plod off me. They were all set to give me a bad time over that. Collusion with Charlie Benson. And worse.'

'I know. But it wasn't true. So I told them.'

There was a pause. He took his big tortoiseshell glasses off and wiped his nose and cheeks with a white handkerchief. Deprived of spectacles, his big bare face had a defenceless look, exposed and pale, as though daylight rarely reached it.

'My aunt Mabel now,' he said, polishing his spectacles with the white handkerchief, 'she came from Sydenham.'

'Oh, really? Did she?'

'She did. And I'll tell you something else. She taught me all I knew about art when I was a lad. Dead proud of Sydenham, she was.'

'Was she? I suppose Pissarro painted her, did he, walking home from church or something?'

He gave me a very sharp look. 'I'm not that bloody old, Simpson. And nor was my aunt Mabel. We are talking of Camille, aren't we, not his son Lucien?'

'Oh yes.'

'Well, Camille Pissarro painted in Sydenham and Norwood in the eighteen-seventies, mate, not last week.'

I smiled. 'I know.' The tea had come and I took a sip of it. 'There are quite a lot of those paintings in famous public galleries now.'

'Right. My aunt Mabel used to take me out when I was a lad and show me the places, walk me round the streets

56

where he lived. Anerley Hill and Belvedere Road and all those. I saw some of those paintings long before all that lot—' he jerked a gesticulation in the general direction of Bond Street—'got interested in anything other than Breughel the Elder.' He put his glasses back on. 'I've been interested in Camille Pissarro, man and boy, for longer than I care to think about. All down to my aunt Mabel. She was a lot more Jewish than we were and took a pride in Pissarro. I mean, once she'd started me off, then I was into all the Chelsea boys, Whistler and the Greaves, Sargent and John and the whole of Tite Street, but you can't buy them now, except for the Greaves and some of the Johns, not with my capital, anyway.'

'What about Pissarro, then?'

'Ah.' He gave me a cunning look. 'That depends. If I knew I had a genuine buyer—a genuine buyer, mind, not just a looker—I might take the plunge on a Pissarro. If not, I'd buy it on—on a consideration, should I say?'

'That would be perfectly acceptable to us.'

He grunted. 'Talk just like a banker, don't you? You might not agree what a suitable consideration would be. After all, the Sydenham Avenue painting fetched a record when the National Gallery bought it at Christie's sale. Back in 1984.'

'Oh, we'd stand by our word once we'd given it.'

'What if I found a Pissarro for you and you wouldn't buy it? If you didn't like the price or if the colours didn't match the carpet at the Bank?'

I thought carefully. 'If it was the sort of Pissarro we'd commissioned you to find and, then, for some reason, we didn't buy it, even though it was genuine, I think we'd pay reasonable out-of-pocket expenses until it could be sold on. This seems an unlikely possibility to me, though.'

'Hm. I'll think about that.' A note of sarcasm came into his voice. 'Is that all you're interested in just now? A Pissarro, painted in England?'

'That and a Monet.'

For a moment he checked. Then he put back his head and brayed, glasses flashing with reflected light. 'Is that all?

A Monet? Har! You're a bit ambitious, aren't you? What, like the one in Trafalgar Square? Got a few million to use up, have you?'

I grinned at him this time. 'No, we haven't. And to be honest, I don't think we'll find one. The Pissarro is more likely and even that, I fully understand, won't come easy. But if you find one and it's the right sort, we can come to an arrangement with you. I'm sure of that.'

Just then the doorbell rang as someone entered the gallery. He turned quickly, pulled a book aside on one of the shelves above his desk, and peered through what was evidently a one-way mirror.

'Huh. A possible customer. Wealthy-looking woman. Excuse me a sec. Never can tell.'

'Of course. Business before pleasure.'

He leered at me and disappeared through the office door. I heard him adopt the refined tones of the fine art salesman as he approached the visitor and then the automatic sealer closed off the door. I got up to stretch my legs and peered at the Harold Harvey, trying to make out how much of it was original. It had been relined, which pulled it together considerably, and I noticed that it wasn't a wax reline, which has gone out of fashion these days, because of wax filling the impasto, so it must have been a light glue of some sort.

Morris Goldsworth came back into the room, muttering.

'No sale?'

'Dorothea Sharp,' he mimicked the high pipe of an upper-class woman. 'Haven't you got a good Dorothea Sharp?' His tone changed. 'Bloody Dorothea Sharp. Children on beaches, painted by numbers. I remember when Dorothea Sharps were five hundred quid, not five thousand.'

'And ten thousand. And, I've heard, up to seventy thousand.'

'Ridiculous! There's too much money chasing that fashionable gear.' He waved a hand towards his gallery. 'I could sell them some real paintings for seventy thousand. What are you looking at?'

58

'Is this a good Harold Harvey?'

'Not for you, it isn't.'

'Why not?'

He grunted. 'Because it isn't a Harold Harvey.'

'What?'

'It's a fake. I was done good and proper on that one. Greed, of course. Tucked me up. I was greedy. Thought I was getting a bargain. Signed and dated. Tucked me up good and proper. I hang it there to teach me a lesson.'

'Oh dear.'

He adjusted his big spectacles for a moment and then peered at me. 'Listen, Mr Tim Simpson, banker; we are talking of more than half a million quid at minimum, you do realize that? Just to come under starter's orders? Possibly a million? Eh?'

'Oh, sure, Morris. I realize that.'

'I mean, he's supposed to have painted exactly twelve paintings in that area back in 1870 and 1871. Only one of them, supposedly, is missing or unaccounted for. Myself, I don't believe it. I think a lot of art gets lost from artists' studios. All of 'em are the same. These art historians can never really trace all a man's work.' Contempt came into his voice again. 'Art experts. Anyone who's been in the trade knows there ain't any such thing.'

'True.'

'But that period—the 1870s—was Pissarro's greatest, according to his old mate Cézanne. So you'd better brace yourself if I get wind of something.'

'I will.'

'The 1890s stuff—Charing Cross Bridge—isn't exactly cheap, either. The pointillist stuff.'

The doorbell rang again. Morris Goldsworth turned to look through his one-way mirror.

'Good God,' he said. 'Two whole customers in one afternoon. I'll get blood pressure if this goes on.'

I grinned. 'I'd better leave you, Morris. Business is business.'

'OK. I'll be in touch. You can believe that.'

'Right-ho.' I held out my hand and he shook it. The first

59

time I'd ever shaken hands with Morris Goldsworth. It just shows what a love of art can do for you.

It wasn't until I was out on the pavement, mingling with those heading for the stations and their suburban homes, that I remembered that I'd forgotten to talk to Morris about that other, rather important, matter. I had been so disarmed by Morris's new attitude towards me, sparked no doubt by his desire to be in on the purchase of a painting from what he regarded as his own special territory, that the question had gone clean out of my mind.

CHAPTER 9

The Houseman, as they now call the Beetle and Wedge, wasn't very full at something after seven o'clock. I got there smartly on time because I suspected that Sister Katie Theaker wouldn't be too tolerant of a late showing by me. I bought a pint of bitter and retired to a table to look round. The place had been completely re-done since the days I remember, when it had been a rather genuine, scruffy London pub with varnished tongued-and-grooved panelling half way up the walls and smoked Lincrusta of yellow hue up to the darkened ceiling. It had been opened out somehow, with etched glass panels imposed to convey that mock-Victorian look that pub designers seem to find irresistible nowadays. The effect was antiseptic and impersonal; the cold varnish of reproduction chairs covered in some sort of washable plastic imitation Rexine dispelled any feeling of cosiness and permanence. What it needed, I thought uncharitably, was for four rugger fifteens to hold a Saturday night thrash in it, spilling beer that would strip the varnish off the chairs and tables, and heaving vomit into the unspeakably patterned nylon carpet. I decided, after some gloomy examination, that that was probably what did happen from time to time but that the materials chosen by the brewery were resistant to any form of human weakness.

At seven-thirty precisely the saloon door opened and an

attractive woman came in who, I realized and recognized with shock, was Sister Katie Theaker. I leapt to my feet to meet her. Out of uniform, she had improved enormously. She was modestly dressed—I suppose that a nurse's pay doesn't exactly run to Pierre Cardin or whatever—but had somehow altered her hair and made herself up so that she looked pretty, almost beautiful. High heels, exchanged from flat hospital shoes, made her move towards me in shapely progression. I was impressed and more hopeful than I had been prepared for; only her face, despite its attractive make-up, sent out signals of guarded anticipation, of almost defensive reserve. I shook hands with her carefully.

'Hello.'

'Hello.'

'Er, what can I get you to drink?'

She didn't pause to think. 'Vermouth, dry, with ice and lemon, thanks.'

'Fine. I've got us a table over here.'

She sat down and I got her drink from the bar. She raised the glass, made a slight gesture to me with it and took a sip.

'Ah, that's good. It's been a long day today.'

'How is Nobby?'

She held the glass on the table and looked at me directly, with what I realized was still a professional, not an off-duty, look. 'He's making a little progress. Actually, I think the forecast is getting a little more optimistic. It's still early days, though. There's a long way to go.'

'Thank God for that. So, despite my efforts of yesterday, he might yet survive?'

She regarded me with that still-professional look, one that held disapproval combined with something else, something unadmiring, then slowly the look changed and the hint of a smile came to her lips, which I noticed were naturally full and humorous, but which had a downward drag to them, as though life's disappointments had temporarily subdued their naturally light-hearted expression.

'What on earth did that,' she said, 'was quite unprecedented. I've never seen anything like it. Do you normally have such a violent effect on him?'

I smiled. 'Not really. Well, not usually. I—'

At that moment the saloon door, across the other side of the bar, opened and a girl came in, followed by Dr Redman. He held the door for her, cheerful of demeanour, and she smiled winningly at him as they approached the bar counter. They looked different out of uniform, both of them, but it was undoubtedly the nurse I'd seen him with in the hospital corridor that same day. He grinned, patted her, and looked up to order drinks from the barman. That was when he saw us.

'My goodness,' I said to Katie Theaker in a low voice which conveyed totally innocent, ingenuous ignorance of the situation, 'isn't that Dr Redman? I'd better keep out of his sight, I think. I've got an idea that I'm not his favourite person after yesterday.'

Redman had gone absolutely still at the bar. His face, was it just my imagination, had paled. His companion was still chattering brightly. A look of guilt and defiance came over Redman, then anger and irritation. He stared at me in disbelief.

'Yes,' Sister Katie Theaker said, in a bright unemotional voice that conveyed total disinterest under which total involvement simmered, 'why, yes, that is Tony Redman. I shouldn't worry if I were you. He's got a lot of cases on his hands and one little upset won't bother him.'

The girl had seen us now and had stopped chattering. Redman was paying for drinks mechanically, counting out coins and flashing glances up towards us.

'Oh good,' I said bluffly, 'no harm done, then.'

She wasn't listening. She had set herself about, holding a pose and touching the back of her hair. The careful and attractive make-up, I thought with a twinge of sadness, hadn't been for my benefit at all. She had known who would be coming here. She turned towards me now, with a bright attentive expression of the sort a woman uses to show the world that she is absolutely captivated and entranced by the conversation she is having with her companion, who is someone she is madly attracted to. I can put up with this, I thought, I can put up with this for Nobby's sake; nothing else.

'What?' she asked, smiling brightly. 'What did you say?'

'I was saying,' I lied, 'that I don't usually have that effect on Nobby. Usually he tries to dismember me with the nearest weapon he can find.'

She laughed, a bright, forced, society-induced laugh, totally false, her eyes flashing at me. Then she leant forward to put her hand on my arm in an affectionate and impulsive gesture of approval. It was bad luck on Redman; he had just left the bar to go to a table and he caught the full impact of it as he looked down the line of the bar angle to see us. He didn't actually spill either of the drinks he was carrying and you couldn't actually hear the grinding of his teeth, but it must have been a near thing. He sat down abruptly at his table and Sister Theaker took her hand off my arm.

'Nobby and I are old friends,' I said. 'We played rugger together. He is a very serious, very dedicated police officer and it affects his sense of humour. I tend to get in his way now and again and he gets very stuffy about it. I suspect that may be the problem now.'

'Get in his way?' She actually had been listening this time. 'Get in his way? How on earth does that come about?'

'Oh, Nobby was on the Art Fraud Squad. I work, part of the time, as an adviser on White's Art Investment Fund. Interests have crossed from time to time. On certain occasions.'

'Art?' She looked at me curiously. 'I would never have associated you with art.'

'Oh? Why not?'

'Well, I suppose Bruno used to go on about your playing rugby, about how you once scored the winning try against Oxford, steamrollering across the line with the entire Oxford pack clinging to you and all that sort of heroically muscular stuff.'

'Bruno? Who on earth is Bruno?'

She stared at me. 'My late, unlamented husband, Mr Saunders. Oh, I see. You called him Bungo. His real name was—is—Bruno.'

'Good God. Bruno? Poor fellow. Was his mother Italian or something?'

She smiled. 'No, she wasn't. And I didn't like her, either. But I do remember now. Bruno said that you were quite unsuitable for a front-row forward, really. The wrong physique and the wrong attitude. But somehow you used to get away with it.'

'Ah, how interesting. That would make a good epitaph, wouldn't it? I can see it carved on my gravestone. "He used to get away with it. Until this time."'

'Well it certainly wouldn't be the right one for me.' Her face had gone back to being serious again. 'Getting away with it is definitely not my forte.' She finished her drink quickly and there was an embarrassing silence. Tactfully not inquiring further, mainly because it was not a line I felt comfortable in pursuing, I got up to get her another drink, staying at the far end of the bar from Redman and his companion, who were now chatting together in relaxed fashion. It seemed to me that a little more lubrication might help Sister Theaker and to a certain extent it did, because when she'd had another swallow she looked at me and said, 'I'm sorry I was a bit frosty this morning. It was your calling me Katie, you see. It took me back. Since I've—since my divorce—I've not been called that. I'm Kate now. I don't use Katie any more.'

'Oh I see. I'm sorry. Er, Kate. May I call you Kate?'

'Of course.'

'Look, um, I don't want to ask you anything unprofessional or anything, but the police don't want me near and Dr Redman obviously thinks that I'm a dangerous nitwit. He's banned me from Nobby's presence. I just wanted to ask you: if Nobby's improving a bit, he's not been talking at all, has he?'

She stared at me, perplexed. 'Talking? Good heavens, no. He's not conscious yet.'

'Oh. Oh dear. I just wondered if he'd given any indication of, well, you know, what happened.'

A guarded look came back into her face, which had been easing up with the effect of the second vermouth. She hesitated, and I spoke again, quickly, to explain. 'Listen, I'm not a criminal or anything. I'm sure you realize that. Nobby is one of my oldest friends. In fact he's the closest I have. I actually owe him my life. I'm not trying to muscle in on a very serious police investigation but his reaction to me was extraordinary. I believe, I believe very powerfully, that something I know or could know might help things. That Brandon bloke has been incredibly obtuse. I've known Nobby for years, know how his mind works, and there could be something, some connection, that would make yesterday make sense. It may be something quite innocuous, some small clue, anything. But I think it should be pursued. It might help.'

Her face softened a little. She had a smooth skin, rather fair and thick, that showed few wrinkles, and I reflected that she was one of those women who were lucky, who would age well if too much disappointment or too much bitterness didn't spoil the line of the mouth by dragging it down.

'Your doctor's obviously biased against me, too,' I said, turning now to a little underhand politicking, 'despite Gillian Roberts wanting me to stay by Nobby. I think it's ridiculous. I would have been prepared to sit quite quietly beside him and listen, but now I'm out in the cold.'

She fingered her glass. 'Well,' she said. 'I don't know. Quite honestly I'm not supposed to say anything. But it's not as though there has been anything to give away. I mean, there's been the odd word, you get that with his condition. Because—because he's in the condition he's in, it's nearly all incoherent, obviously. There was one, I don't think it can do any harm to tell you. Woods. Or wood. That's all I've heard during my stints with him.'

'Woods?'

'Yes. Woods. They listen to him all the time. He called it out, several times. Woods. But that's all while I've been there. He has nursing on a twenty-four-hour basis, of course. And guards. There was one lot who said they were all off to Mitcham.'

'Mitcham?'

65

'Yes. Some sort of search, I believe. But you mustn't tell anyone. It's very hush-hush, of course.'

'I thought he was brought in from Dulwich?'

'He was. From Dulwich Hospital. But that's where they all shot off to. Mitcham. From something he's supposed to have said. I don't think there are any woods in Mitcham, are there? I mean, I've been to Mitcham Common, but I've never heard of Mitcham Woods. Have you?'

The scene inside the pub had gone frozen, congealed. My heart had stopped. My vision was somehow reverse-telescoped so that my hands, on the table near my beer, looked very small and a long way off.

'I say, are you all right? You've gone very pale.'

Now I saw her face, concerned in a mild way, looking at me. I made a physical effort and smiled. 'No, I haven't heard of a Mitcham Woods. Never.' There was nothing I could do about the condition that had arrived until the following day. Nothing. I thought it over and made sure. I shook my head gently to myself, became aware that she was watching me, and grinned.

'Sorry. I'm all right. My condition must be hunger, I think.'

'Hunger?'

'Sure. I didn't have lunch today. Normally I would have eaten by now. It must be after eight, isn't it? By this time I've already normally had my little bit of sustenance of some sort if I've missed lunch. I know: there's a small French restaurant near here that's supposed to be very good. La Cuisine, it's called. I've never tried it but everyone says it's excellent. Would you like something to eat? We could nip over there for a bite. No nonsense; just a meal?'

She stared at me. 'La Cuisine? But that's frightfully expensive.'

'Is it? But it's very good, they all say. And we have our health to consider. Can't just nip into the nearest curry house, can we?'

'Aren't you—excuse me—aren't you expected or anything?'

'Expected? Me? Oh, I see. You mean Sue, yesterday. Ah.

66

No, I'm not expected. We aren't, er, we used to be, but it isn't—I mean—I'm not expected. By anyone. Quite free. Like you, I divorced a while ago and the knot has never been retied. Sue's an old friend of the Roberts's too, of course.' I put on one of those objective sorts of expressions to match the tone of my voice. 'Sue Westerman is looking after Gillian Roberts during this very bad time. The two children, you know.'

'Oh.' She looked down at the table. Then her inflection changed radically. 'Oh. I thought—oh. I see.'

'What about it? I'm starving.'

'La Cuisine.' Her voice was wondering. 'I don't think I've ever been to a restaurant as expensive as that, ever.'

'Splendid.' I got to my feet. 'If we go now we'll miss the late rush.'

She got up cheerfully. A look of sheer duplicity crossed her face. She preceded me down the bar and, as we passed near the table where Redman and his companion were sitting, she turned to put her arm confidentially in mine.

'La Cuisine,' she said, in a voice that would carry just far enough. 'What a great idea, Tim.'

I had my back to Redman all the way to the door. It took a real effort not to look round over my shoulder. If doctors carried their scalpels out of work I had no doubt that one would have been buried between my shoulder-blades. It was a massive relief to get out on to the pavement and hail a passing taxi.

Kate Theaker took her arm away as I opened the taxi door. Her face straightened seriously. 'This is very nice of you, Tim. There's just one thing I ought to let you know; I wouldn't like you to get the wrong impression.'

I held up my hand. 'Don't tell me, let me guess. You don't make a habit out of this sort of thing?'

As she got into the cab I heard her laugh, the first real, genuine laugh I'd had out of her that evening.

CHAPTER 10

In the morning I got the car out and drove to a place near Gunnersbury Park. Not far away, traffic thundered by on the M4, heading out towards Heathrow. It was a nondescript area of small, light industry, sports grounds and factories. Railway lines threaded through it, carrying silver tubes of Underground trains that emerged blinking above ground somewhere near Hammersmith and unconvincingly tried to look at ease in their exposed condition. Down to the side of one railway line, built up against a rusting chain-link fence held on flaking concrete posts, was a row of lock-up garages leading to a series of workshops fitted under the arches of a viaduct. Most of the activity was in car repairs, bodywork spraying and panel-beating, but there was a toy distributor and an upholsterers as well. Next to them, one line of garages had been sealed and entrance could only be effected by a single door cut into one of them.

The reliner wore a long white coat. Inside the garages the dividing walls had been removed so that his relining tables could be placed comfortably in the longer spaces provided. He had five tables, all big, each with its flat, stainless steel top under which electrical elements provided the heat, and all with vacuum pumps. Heater controls were mounted on the side of each table; they were all covered in transparent plastic sheeting, under which squares and rectangles of brown canvas could be seen. Along one wall were racks full of canvases. Stacked on another clean wooden table was a pile of paintings, all sliced off their stretchers, all face down. A young lad in a white coat was cleaning the back of one of them with a bottle of solution. The reliner's wife sat at a desk in the corner, typing. Near her, a pot of glue simmered on a thermostatic heater.

The reliner had thick grey hair, carefully waved, and very clean hands. From the breast pocket of his white coat protruded two pens, a plastic ruler and the clip of a magnifying-glass. He might have been a foreman-inspector in an aircraft factory, about to apply his micrometer to a suspect alloy component. The reliner was a technician, a man much versed in materials and their properties, in temperatures and timescales, in ageing and the bad habits of canvas preparation used by artists going back for four hundred years. He stood in front of me now, not liking the way my gaze kept flicking round the room, taking in the odd painting which was not face down. The reliner was a very circumspect man, very discreet. He worked for several West End galleries and was very cautious about the work-in-progress about him, quite apart from the fact that his premises were uninsured. The premium on a Botticelli left for a few weeks in these conditions would have been commercially ruinous.

At my question a little relief came into his face. 'Oh,' he said. 'Oh. Got some work for him, have you?'

'Yes. We used him before, you know.'

The reliner nodded gravely. 'I remember,' he said. 'A Stanhope Forbes, wasn't it?'

'It was. My goodness, you've got a good memory.'

The reliner smiled condescendingly. It was the reliner's business to remember such things, to play the unending game of Pelmanism that is the antiques and art trade. Somewhere deep in the reliner's premises, or perhaps locked away at his home, there would be carefully-preserved files of photographs of thousands of canvases, showing the paintings both before restoration and after. The reliner was methodical and painstaking, a technical sort of man whose precautions were wise; accusations about damage done to paintings or their alteration could only be refuted by hard evidence.

The reliner opened his mouth, closed it, and then opened it again to speak cautiously. 'I can give you his home address,' he said. 'I'm afraid he keeps the studio details very close to his chest. And, of course, he's moved since you last went to him.'

'Indeed.'

A vaguely disturbed look came to the reliner's face. 'I

69

was sorry to hear about that trouble,' he said. 'He fell on hard times for a while. But he seems to be doing all right now.'

'Oh good. Is he giving you much work?'

The reliner's eyes flickered. 'Not much. Occasionally. But not a lot.'

'Oh. I wasn't meaning to pry, sorry. Just wondered how he was doing, that's all.'

The reliner nodded. Still barring my way, he turned to call over his shoulder to his wife, who had been listening intently whilst rustling a pile of invoices through her typewriter. 'Vicky—have you got his address there? Home address, that is?'

She looked up, pretending to pay attention for the first time. 'Brondesbury Park,' she said, 'not far from the cemetery—Willesden Lane—going towards Kilburn High Road. One of those roads going through.' She rummaged in a drawer. 'Here you are—off Carlisle Road.' She gave a name and number. 'Think he has a flat there, ground floor. Their kid must be about seven, now.'

I nodded. 'Time flies. Seems only yesterday he was in a pushchair. Thanks very much to both of you.'

'A pleasure, Mr Simpson.' The reliner stared at me. 'Is your Fund doing much restoration work now?'

'Oh, er, a bit, you know. Not a lot. But now and then.'

'You'll keep us in mind, I hope?'

'Of course. Absolutely. Nothing but the best. And the most discreet.'

'Thank you.'

I crunched back outside to where I'd parked my Jaguar. A paint-sprayed lad from one of the railway arches was eyeing it as he sipped a mug of tea, sitting on a wooden box in the cool grey morning air. Nearby, a hand-held grinder shrieked against a chassis frame and sparks showered from a welder. Vans were being loaded outside the toy distributors. Behind the reliner's gravely closed doors, old canvases were being pressed warmly and moistly on to new canvases, the flakes of paint on one side re-settling themselves back into gesso preparation that had softened with the years. Not exactly a Risorgimento scene but a busy one none the less, and all the better for that. I got into the car and headed for Brondesbury Park.

The street was nondescript and the house wasn't particularly old. At the front door there were two bells and I pressed the lower one and waited. A child's call came from within. After a while the door opened, on a chain, and a woman's face peered out. Below her a small boy pressed a rather sticky face into the gap.

'Hello—is Mitch in?'

The woman's eyes narrowed a bit and she shook her head. 'No. He's out at work.'

'Oh dear. Can I get hold of him there?'

She frowned, and then a look of recognition came into her face. 'Oh!' she said. 'It's Mr—er—Mr—I'm sorry, I've forgotten your name, but I do remember your face.'

'Simpson. Tim Simpson. From White's Art Fund.'

'Of course! Hold on.' The door shut, nearly guillotining the small boy's nose, and then opened again. The woman was small and dark, tired-looking but with curly hair and a button nose. She wore a flowered apron over a sweater and stained jeans. She smiled at me and the boy grabbed her leg to hold her, shyly. I held out my hand and she shook it. 'I'm sorry. I've got a terrible memory for names, but I remember you. You gave him that work two or three years ago.'

'That's right. I was wanting to contact him again.'

'Oh. Well, of course. I know he liked working on your stuff.'

What she meant was that we paid good money, we weren't mean like the West End boys.

'Can I find him at his studio?'

'Oh. Well.' Her face crinkled for a moment and then cleared again. 'I'm not supposed to, but I'm sure it'd be all right for you. Fact, he'd be cross if I let you pass without seeing him. But usually it's no visitors at the studio, see?'

'Of course. I understand. But I'd be sorry to miss him. I need to talk this one through with him. It's an interesting job.'

71

'All right. It's not far. I'll get a bit of paper and give you directions. Hang on.'

She disentangled the boy and disappeared down a passage that led to the kitchen. The boy peered up at me shyly.

'Hello, sonny. What's your name?'

'Jeff,' he said breathlessly.

He was one of those thin small pale boys with grey-blue eyes and muddy-coloured hair that you see everywhere in London. He stared at me fixedly, rather disconcertingly concentrating on my broken nose, which suddenly felt conspicuous.

'Shouldn't you be at school or something?'

A look of indignation came over his face. 'It's me 'olidays,' he protested.

'Oh. I'm sorry, of course. Holidays are not bad, eh?'

'They're all right,' he said. 'I was going out wiv me dad today but he had to go to work. Geezer phoned him up and he had to go.'

'Oh dear. Where were you going?'

'Fishing. Up the reservoir.'

'Ah. Well, I expect he'll take you when he's finished.'

'Yeah.'

His mother emerged with a strip of paper. 'Off Kilburn High Road,' she said. 'There's a couple of old studios there. He has the top one.'

'Right. Thanks very much.'

'All right.' She smiled at me. 'Goodbye.'

''Bye.' I smiled back at her and then at the boy, who grinned suddenly before ducking behind his mother again.

Back to the car, down a few streets, into Irish territory, across Kilburn High Road and down another street I went. There, built into a terrace, was a tall house with very large windows on the first and second floors. I parked further down the street and got out. For a moment I stopped and leant against the car.

Only two days ago—was it really only two days ago?— I had been living peacefully with Sue Westerman in my flat in Onslow Gardens. Then there'd been the telephone call, first thing in the morning, taking events completely out of hand. Nobby Roberts was smashed up in hospital, still unconscious. I'd had a row with Commander Brandon. Sue had left me. Jeremy had commissioned me to find a Monet and a Pissarro. Sam Johnson and Charles Massenaux thought I was mad. I'd taken a nurse out to dinner for the first time in many years, started to come to terms with Morris Goldsworth, and was now standing in a street off the Kilburn High Road, about to visit a restorer's studio in search of I didn't know what. All in two days? It was time to get a grip on things; these instincts, these hunch-pursuits, had to come to something or else be jettisoned.

The house was divided, floor by floor, with a common staircase that had once been the handsome main staircase of a residential dwelling, the landings now partitioned off to form flats and working studios. At the top, I headed for the door giving to the front studio, the one that would have a large window. It was a modern, hardboarded door in the partition, painted cream like the rest. I knocked politely, but there was no answer.

I knocked again twice. There was no name on the door and no number. I checked the slip of paper in my hand. This was the right place. I turned the handle and went in. No one called out so I moved cautiously into the room, taking in the clutter that littered it. An easel stood to one side of the window, a working easel with small clods of oil paint, multicoloured, splashed on it. A big table in the middle of the room was sprinkled with paint tubes, brushes in jars, acrylics, papers, sketches, string and drawing instruments. A bottle of Scrubbs Cloudy Ammonia caught my eye, then a gaggle of other bottles containing solvents, a brown screw-top jar of acetone, various soap solutions, Vim, a nail brush and several badly-bristled toothbrushes. The working trappings of a picture restorer. On the far wall was a sink with two taps and a draining-board. Under the central table was a folio chest and another folio chest with long, deep drawers stood next to the sink. On it was a pile of books, carelessly stacked, mostly art reference books or coffee-table books that would be lavishly illustrated, but some biographies as well. I caught sight of Holroyd's

Augustus John and two of Hesketh Pearson's, *The Man Whistler* and *Conan Doyle*, the latter in a cheap postwar edition by Guild Books. That gave me a pang because Nobby Roberts had always been a keen Doyle fan, way back when we were at college together. There were two lavish Swiss books by Skira, one on the Impressionists and the other on prints. Plenty of material for a restorer to check against but, oddly, no paintings, either on the easel or stacked anywhere else that I could see. Did the restorer have no work in progress? I turned to look further into the room.

Against the back wall, away from the light, was an oak office desk littered with papers that looked as though someone had been searching for something. Between the central table and the office desk was an overturned chair and, lying by the chair, was the head of a man with his mouth open.

I caught the edge of the central table to steady myself. The man was lying face down and his dark, greying hair, going a little thin at the back, hung down in stripes over the visible side of his face. He was wearing a sweater and a dark shirt. One hand was thrown out beside his head; the other was pinned under him. Blood had seeped out from under his chest but not in any large quantity, just a stain that spread briefly over the dirty carpet on the floor. As I moved cautiously round the table I saw that he was wearing jeans. Very carefully I bent down to get as near as I could without touching anything. He was dead, right enough; I guessed that he had been shot. I thought of the little boy waiting to go fishing and of the wife in her flowered apron, giving me the slip of paper.

Two men came through the studio door very quietly, with hardly a creak of shoe leather. I whirled round and straightened but they were standing against the light and, for a moment, I was unsighted. Before I could crouch to defend myself one of them held up a card, a card I couldn't see against the light.

'We are police officers,' he said in a hard formal tone, bracing himself carefully so that, then, I knew he was unarmed. 'Who the hell are you?'

74

The second one stepped sideways away from the window and, blinking, I now saw his clean fawn raincoat, his white shirt, and his unmistakable brown tie.

'Jesus Christ,' he said.

I relaxed carefully, starting to feel the shock make my legs tremble. I would have to sit down in a few seconds; shock does that to you.

'Hello, Sam,' I said. 'How are you? I'm afraid we've all been a bit slow off the mark.' I stood aside to let them see the form on the carpet. 'Someone has been to see Mitch Woods before us. And murdered him.'

CHAPTER 11

During a brief visit to San Francisco, three or four years ago, I was having a drink outside the Embarcadero Center after doing some business for the Bank when a band came up to play to the crowded bar. It was a group called Mitch Woods and his Rocket 88s. I remember being amused by the choice of a future year and I liked the band but, most striking, the name stuck in my head because it was the same as that of a restorer in North London who we'd used to spruce up one or two paintings for the Art Fund. I suppose that Mitch was short for Mitchell in the restorer's case—certainly not for Mitcham anyway—and he was nothing like the San Francisco bandleader, nor did he like rock music but he, too, was amused when I told him about it. Our Mitch Woods was a normal, almost nondescript sort of man of medium build and dark hair who terrified the art trade by his ability at restoration and the styles he could paint in, particularly the ever-popular Impressionists, Post-Impressionists and Expressionists like Manet, Cézanne and Vlaminck.

I thought about this as the group assembled round the plain table in the police station interview room and sat down opposite me. They had put me at one end so they could all face me. It was three hours since I'd found Mitch

Woods murdered in his studio. None of them looked friendly. Commander Brandon of Scotland Yard appeared to be particularly put out, as though he'd had an ace trumped by a tinhorn. Sam Johnson was in a bad temper. The local CID man, a sergeant, eyed me with hostility. A fourth man, better dressed, looked blank.

Brandon focused a glare on me. 'Your position is very serious. Very serious indeed. You were warned, specifically warned, to avoid involvement in this matter. Now you are a suspect. Your arrest will follow.'

'Oh really? I shall wait to hear you give the usual warning then, before I hear the charge and before making my statutory telephone call to Sandy McGuire.'

The local CID man scowled. 'Who's Sandy McGuire?'

I smiled at him unpleasantly. 'Sandy McGuire is a senior partner in Bernson, Holman and McGuire, solicitors to White's Bank. His reputation in such matters is considerable.' I fixed an accusing stare on Brandon. 'What he will do to you if you arrest me will beggar description. Your career will be destroyed. I shall advise him, in particular, to concentrate on letting the world know that, by refusing me access to Nobby Roberts or to any information about him, you allowed the murder of a key witness to occur when adequate protection should have been afforded to him.'

There was a silence. Brandon licked his lips. The fourth, better-dressed man, who was dark like Sam Johnson, but more saturnine, looked at me curiously.

'How did you come to visit this man Woods? What information did you receive that led you to make your visit? How did you know him, or of him?'

This was tricky. 'Who are you?' I demanded, to get a bit of time to think.

'This,' rasped Brandon, 'is Detective-Inspector Warren of the Drugs Squad.'

'Oh.'

Silence. The four of them stared at me. The most important thing in my mind was not to get Kate Theaker into trouble for dropping the info to me. We'd had a very pleasant dinner at La Cuisine, where she had obviously relished everything about the place and had cheered up considerably by the end of the evening. I had seen her very decorously back to a flat she shared with three other senior nurses and then proceeded home to an empty Onslow Gardens only occupied by thoughts of Sue and how to find Mitch Woods. Nobby's murmurings were obvious to me; poor old Sam Johnson and his gang had taken time to work it out.

'Gillian Roberts,' I said. 'She said that Nobby had mumbled something about wood or woods.' I looked at the table-top and then up at them, directly. 'And there was mention of your going off to Mitcham. I just put two and two together.'

A puzzled frown came to Sam Johnson's face and he stared at me intently. The frown deepened into a scowl. I decided to carry on, quickly.

'In the days when Nobby was in the Art Fraud Squad,' I said, 'it was me who introduced him to Mitch Woods. Four or five years ago, perhaps. I thought it would help Nobby to understand the processes of art restoration. And other things. You see, the big boys in the art trade paid off Mitch Woods once. Made him promise not to produce any more fakes. It was a bit like that chap in Mexico who used to print rare stamps and the stamp dealers paid him to stop it. Quite a lump sum, I believe. Well, the same thing happened with Mitch. It didn't do him any good, because after the excitement of turning out some really hot fakes, going back to restoration was very dull. Mitch was a bit of a joker and a lot of what he did was for the thrill of it as much as for the money. I lost contact with him but there were stories that he'd got on to sniffing cocaine. And other things. Other drugs, I mean.'

Warren sat back slightly but still kept his gaze fixed on me. 'That's very interesting,' he said. 'What sort of fakes did he paint? When he was doing them?'

'Modern French. Late-nineteenth- and twentieth-century French. Where the money is. The valuable stuff. But he did stop completely in return for a pay-off.'

'I see.'

77

'If you had let me sit in with Nobby, if you hadn't had me frozen out of even the entrance to the hospital, I might have been able to tell you all this much earlier.'

The local CID man made an expression of disbelief and anger, leant forward on the table, opened his mouth, caught Warren's eye, closed his mouth again and sat back in his chair. Sam Johnson's face was completely blank. Warren had gone still, deferentially still, after shooting one quick glance at Brandon. For about ten seconds, the room waited.

You do not get to be a Commander at Scotland Yard if you are a bloody fool. I might not have liked Brandon but I didn't underestimate him, despite the dreadful performance he'd given at the hospital. Brandon and I were, obviously, chalk and cheese, or more like cat and dog, but Brandon was a professional, an authoritarian professional maybe, but still a professional. The involvement of people like me was a real pain to Brandon. I had no doubt what his position on merchant banking would be, either; rather to the right of Nobby Roberts, who regarded my profession as one pursued by total parasites. Brandon cleared his throat.

'I regret that I seem to have made an error of judgement.' His voice was calm, as though making a recital, and he fixed me with a clear stare. 'As it happened, possibly a serious error. Chief Inspector Roberts has been a close colleague and an assistant of mine for a considerable period. I allowed my distress at his condition to impair my professional detachment. What I should have done, of course, was to have asked you to provide us with any information that might have been of assistance. Your long, er, acquaintanceship with Roberts could have clarified certain clues which took us much longer to follow up. Mitcham and woods were a case in point. When, however, you also reacted so strongly at the hospital—quite understandably in view of your concern—my own initial reaction was to prevent a very serious investigation being complicated by external emotional factors. I over-reacted. The effect your visit had on Roberts was in part to blame. Nevertheless, I was mistaken. I withdraw unreservedly any remarks I may have made at the time which may have given offence to you. In view of your clear desire to see that justice is done and your very special knowledge of certain aspects of Roberts's activities, I would ask you, now, to give your full assistance and collaboration to the officers investigating this case.'

He paused for a moment. This was handsome stuff, very handsome, especially in front of his juniors, and I opened my mouth to answer, but he held up a hand.

'The only caveat I will make,' he continued, 'is that your assistance, as I say, should be carried out in full cooperation with my officers. That there shall be no idea of pursuing private personal revenge or of precipitate action. As it happens, I think it unlikely that the, er, the other aspects of this case, particularly Detective-Inspector Warren's investigations, will impinge on what might have been Roberts's involvement. But that remains to be seen. We would appreciate your help in providing any information we cannot obtain easily through our normal procedures.'

My goodness, I thought, fancy admitting that I might be able to help. I nodded, looking back at him. 'You will have it. And I have to say that my behaviour at the hospital was as much to blame as any reaction of yours. I was upset. Your position demanded that you issued the warnings you did and I apologize for my intolerant attitude and actions. I didn't help. I am willing to do so now.'

Sam Johnson let his blank expression relax. The local CID man blinked. Warren of the Drugs Squad put his hands on the edge of the table, visibly relieved.

'Perhaps we could all have some tea?' he queried, raising his eyebrows at no one in particular.

'Good idea,' said Brandon.

The local CID sergeant leapt to the door to issue instructions and there was a general scraping of chairs in relief and relaxation. The temperature went up a few degrees. For want of something to say and to cover Sam Johnson's revelations to me in the pub two days earlier I spoke to Warren, assuming an air of innocence.

'Do I take it that your presence means that Nobby was working on a drugs investigation?'

Warren nodded, cautiously. 'He was covering certain

aspects of an extensive and, I might add, very secret investigation into what we believe is a widespread network of drug-dealing. He had not been involved for very long.'

'So his Art Fraud background was not particularly relevant, then?'

Warren frowned. 'That's an important and seemingly difficult question now. Initially no, it wasn't. I mean, he wasn't coopted on to the team because of that knowledge, not at all. And there was no suggestion of any need for such knowledge. He was working on the cash flow aspects, actually—' he shot a glance at me— 'in banking and so forth. Although part of a team, his work was independent. He reported at regular intervals to me as project coordinator. He was due to have an extensive session with us today.' He looked at Brandon. 'I think that what I have told Mr Simpson doesn't cross the boundaries of what is absolutely secret but gives him a reasonable background.'

Brandon nodded weightily. 'No problem, Warren. I think it fair to tell you, Simpson, that we were not looking for any, er, artistic involvement. For that reason, perhaps, it took us time to deduce the Woods connection. We still don't know what Woods had to do with all this, but your information that Woods may have been an addict is important. If he was, our pathologist will tell us, of course, but the sooner we have such intimations the better. Why Roberts should have been speaking Woods's name is something we don't know. It's the first mention of him in this whole investigation and what importance or relevance he has will have to be discovered. As soon as possible. He obviously has great importance, certainly enough for someone to murder him, so Roberts must have found something.'

'How is Nobby? Any nearer consciousness?'

Brandon shook his head. 'I regret to say not. And that Dr Redman is insistent that he be kept absolutelys undisturbed and quiet. Obviously, with a patient so severely injured he is refusing to take any further chances. We are maintaining strict surveillance and waiting in hope. But visitors apart from his wife, are not allowed at present for medical reasons.' He puckered his face. 'It's still touch and go in many ways. A lot could go wrong, according to Redman. I am having to proceed on the basis that we cannot expect anything from Roberts by way of further information, not at present, unless he happens to say something in his current condition. The murder of Woods is an entirely new angle and it will open up new lines of investigation. The rest of the inquiry goes on.' He downed the rest of the tea he had been sipping and began to gather up his files. From the absence of any further curiosity towards me on his part, I began to feel that somewhere, mentally, he was writing my latest involvement off as a coincidence, something that he didn't want to divert him from a more important occupation. He had done his job, squared up the hospital incident, neutralized me and could leave his deputies to act as banderilleros around me, subordinate to his role as matador when needed. He adopted an air of finality. 'I have to go. I would be obliged if you could give these officers any information you think to be relevant. They are in charge of the project on a day-to-day basis and report to me at regular intervals.' He nodded at Warren. 'We'll meet as planned,' he said. Then he turned back to look at me again. 'Thank you,' he said. It cost him, it took him an effort, but he said it. Then he was off, plunging through the door in a large, well-tailored surge of energy that left the room feeling somewhat depleted.

The other three men stared at each other in total hush for a few seconds. Then Sam Johnson blew air from his lungs in a great outward gust and Warren grinned at him in understanding before turning to me. 'Never seen that before,' he said. 'Never. Have some more tea?'

'Thanks. Never seen what before?'

'Brandon apologized. A first, that must be.'

'I'll say.' Sam Johnson shoved his cup across too. 'Bullnose Brandon, they call him at the Yard.' He turned to the local CID man. 'You've just seen history, you have.'

The CID man shook his head. 'What was all that about?'

'He—' Sam Johnson pointed at me— 'had a right set-to with the Commander at the hospital. In irons, he should be. Jabbing him with a forefinger in a manner likely to justify at least a GBH charge, I'd say. Certainly one of malicious assault at minimum. And instead he gets an apology. Mind you—' he shook his head at me— 'it wasn't very nice of you to threaten him with Sandy McGuire. Not nice at all, that wasn't. Not Sandy McGuire.'

'Well, he was threatening me. With arrest.'

'Oh well—that's normal.'

'Par for the course,' the CID man said.

'Just a normal precaution.' Warren smiled bleakly. 'Until we knew you were supposed to be one of us.'

'Oh, very nice. One minute out with the cuffs, the next it's a nice pot of tea and some fairy cakes for the gentleman, sergeant.'

'Pavlovian,' Sam Johnson said. 'Always works.'

'Bugger you, Inspector.'

Sam Johnson smiled. A long wide smile, a meaning smile that I didn't like the look of. 'We've got your statement and we'll go over everything we know again in a minute. So that's all right. I don't think any of us knows too much at the moment. There's just one thing, however, Mr Tim Simpson.'

'What's that?'

The smile came back again and the other two men leant forward interestedly as Sam Johnson spoke. 'I do hope you are going to collaborate with us as the Commander said? Wholeheartedly and openly? No private shenanigans?'

'Of course. Whatever do you mean?'

The smile widened. 'You said that Gillian Roberts told you about the Woods-Mitcham remarks of Nobby's?'

'Yes.'

He leant forward. 'You haven't seen Mrs Roberts since your row with Brandon at the hospital. Nobby hadn't mentioned Woods before then. So she couldn't have told you.'

'There are such things as telephones, you know, Sam.'

'Indeed there are. But you haven't used one. Not to Mrs Roberts. She's under constant surveillance for her protection. And that includes her phone. You haven't spoken to her.'

'Er, well, Sue you know, she's been staying with Gillian. It must have been her.'

'Miss Westerman has taken up residence with Mrs Roberts, certainly. Very kind of her. It's relieved one of our WPCs from looking after her. But you haven't spoken to Miss Westerman, either. Not since she left you the day before yesterday.'

'Eh?'

'The day before yesterday. That was when she left you.' He sighed. 'My constable at the hospital foyer was very impressed. He says you pulled one of the most attractive nursing sisters in the place just like that. Took her out for a noggin and a tuck-in at a classy French restaurant. A particular nursing sister, it was.'

'Oh?'

'News travels, young Tim. News travels. And we have an interest in any staff who are attending to Nobby Roberts.'

'Oh. Er, well, er, I say, look here, Sam, I—you know— you've got it all wrong, I was just—'

He shook his head sadly. 'I think we'd better go over your statement again. You haven't changed at all.' He gave me a meaningful leer. 'No, you haven't changed at all.'

CHAPTER 12

The Westminster Public Reference Library is just off the south side of Leicester Square. St Martin's Street, not Lane, is rather a short lost bit of a street that goes down to Trafalgar Square west of the National Gallery. The library is a very good one on three floors and the great merit of it to me is that the entire top floor is an Art Reference Library with a very good collection of factual stuff. The room isn't particularly large, rather long and narrow in fact, with rows of tables four abreast and small hard wooden chairs for you to sit on while you do your research. You get an odd collection of bods in there, mainly art students digging up material for essays, foreign tourists of intellectual mien, the occasional suburbanite or business man, housewifely-looking women from Hampstead Garden Suburb and that sort of thing. In the accepted manner of Public Library Reference Rooms, everyone studiously ignores everyone else no matter how bizarre their get-up. I've often thought that if a naked woman walked into the Reference Library the librarian would make her wait her turn and fill in her request form before asking her to do anything about modesty. Everyone else would pretend that she didn't exist. In a library, it's anything to avoid a scene.

In front of me I had the first volume of Daniel Wildenstein's *Biographie et Catalogue Raisonnée* of Monet, published by *La Bibliothèque des Arts*, Lausanne & Paris, a large, flat, blue cloth book which came out in different volumes between 1974 and 1985. It's entirely in French, so I blessed my luck that I wasn't too rusty in that language. The bit I was looking at dealt with Monet's sojourn in England during the Franco-Prussian War of 1870–71 and it was all good, factual stuff about such events as the meeting with Durand-Ruel the art dealer, who had a gallery at 168 New Bond Street and the friendship and meeting with Pissarro, who was living close to relatives in Norwood. Monet's address in London was given: 11 Arundel Street, now 7–14 Coventry Street. Things like that. A list of five oil paintings he produced during his stay here was duly illustrated in the rear section of the book:

The Thames and Houses of Parliament, now in the National Gallery, London
Green Park, now in Philadelphia
Hyde Park, now in Providence, Rhode Island
The Pool of London
Boats and the Pool of London

The last two paintings were of shore scenes of the Thames, with beached boats near the houses down towards Whistler's old territory, possibly even influenced by him. The book didn't say where these two paintings were now. Both Monet and Pissarro submitted paintings to the Royal Academy

84

during their stay in England and both were, predictably, refused. They did exhibit at the Exhibition Internationale des Beaux Arts while they were here and Monet had two paintings in that, marine paintings, besides three titled canvases—*Meditation, Camille*, and *Repose*. The book said that he left in May 1871, leaving some canvases behind. End of that particular visit to London.

So what? I blinked at the page in front of me. Now what was I going to do? Around me, chairs creaked as others took notes or there were shufflings as researchers squeezed between tables and shelves to get to the card-index table. What use was the information to me? It was interesting enough, but hardly likely to lead me to a recumbent Monet, lying patiently in wait for me to fall over it. Come to think of it, I hadn't got much idea what the Monet at the National Gallery looked like, and I was only a few hundred yards from it.

'Damn it,' I said, out loud.

The one thing you must not do in a reference library is to talk. Scowls were shot in my direction. The presiding librarian, a thin lady of indeterminate age, peeked over the index chest at me. Silence settled uneasily back on to the gathering. If things had been normal I'd have gone to the Tate, dug Sue out of her basement office, taken her to lunch and sparked some ideas about the Impressionists generally. One of my problems is that I can't get a feel for a subject without prowling round various aspects of it physically, like visiting the place or talking to someone who was involved with it. It's a throwback to my old years as a business consultant, when half the job was chatting up the people involved and the other half involved analysis, at a desk. I had been looking forward to a natter with Mitch Woods, for instance.

Mitch Woods had been murdered, though.

Through the window to my right I could look over the building site where they were preparing the foundations for the extension to the National Gallery, to one of the grand pillared buildings overlooking Trafalgar Square. I supposed that it was Canada House. Beyond it, crossing Cockspur

Street, you can go down an alley by the Two Chairmen pub and see the name of the Grand Trunk Railway of Canada still embossed on the back of a building, the same Grand Trunk Railway of Canada that had as its president one Hays, who cheated Moreton Frewen out of a fortune at Prince Rupert and was drowned on the *Titanic* as a result. That led me to thinking about Moreton Frewen, and Timber Powell's revenge, and Sue, and how stupid all this was. The best thing I could do was to forget all this and make it up with Sue.

My mind was wandering.

While I was sitting there, anonymous and private in a library two floors above the streets of London, policemen were beavering away at Nobby's attempted murder, forensic experts were sifting through Mitch Woods's studio, a pathologist was probably digging into his inert corpse, a WPC—woman police constable—was trying to comfort a flower-aproned bereaved woman with a snub nose and a seven-year-old little boy who was fond of fishing with his dad. There would be dozens of people involved, vast banks of information on tap, all sorts of analytical techniques to be used. But in my *Times* that morning was a report on a killer the police called The Mechanic, who shot a police sergeant dead in 1984 and who wasn't detected until he himself was shot in a car chase four years later. So all that vast apparatus wasn't infallible, didn't have all the answers, couldn't cover every possible aspect of the infinite, cunning, devious machinations of the human criminal let loose in a complex, lightly-controlled society. No computer had my knowledge of Nobby Roberts allied to a series of speculations about Mitch Woods.

'Sod it,' I said, out loud again.

There was a stiff click of tongue from a Burberried lady beside me. I stood up abruptly, closed the Wildenstein volume with a snap and backed away from my table. One or two researchers scowled but the others looked hopeful. Better a noisy departure than an unpredictable presence. I went down the two flights of stone stairs, past the female West Indian who always sits mournfully by the main entrance waiting for book thieves and turned left out along St Martin's Street. A brisk walk in weak October sunshine soon got me to the National Gallery and then I was into its Impressionist room not far from the main entrance. It was time to make contact with the subject, so to speak.

The Monet and the two Pissarros hung on the same wall. The effect was rather gloomy and subdued. The Monet of *The Houses of Parliament and Westminster Bridge* is rather grey, confirming all a Frenchman's conceits about a fog-clouded city. Although the delineation of the nearby jetty is clear and Big Ben is prominent in the background, and a barge or two on the river outline themselves and their red Plimsoll lines unmistakably, the sky and the river are a sort of grey wash and the tones are subdued. The water has those dappled effects Monet used so well in *La Grenouillère*, but the overall effect is dank. Building colour is dark, with little differentiation. The Pissarro paintings are, if anything, more adventurous. I liked the one of *Lower Norwood Effects of Snow*, with its twisting country road and the houses which still exist; to me it seemed strong and vital, very French for all the brown colours, as though Pissarro had seen a landscape of suburban Paris in that winter rural scene south of London. The *Sydenham Road* painting is much more English. Light green grass and a stone church provide a soft, almost watercolour view of a kind that has been plagiarized for decades since. In this painting the house to the left is unmistakably English; you could be nowhere else. I stood back to get a different view and saw, approaching me, a heart-stopping familiar figure in a light-coloured suit and a white blouse.

'Sue!'

She halted in her brisk tracks. For a moment she stared at me incredulously.

'Sue! What luck! What are you doing here?'

Anger flashed across her face. 'You're following me!'

'What?'

'What are you doing here?'

I nearly said I asked you first. It wouldn't have been wise. Sue is a very attractive girl, willowy and smart, a bit

87

businesslike in demeanour and outwardly buttoned-down, but her reactions below are pretty volatile. She doesn't like to bandy words when in a temper and I could see that she wasn't calm.

'I was looking at the Monet and the Pissarros. Why aren't you at the Tate?'

She gave a sort of snort. 'Don't try to be frivolous! Why are you here?'

'I've told you. Looking at them.' I gestured at the wall. 'I—'

'You've no business following me!'

Prickles began to move on my spine. 'I am not following you, Sue. But I am very pleased to see you. Can we talk somewhere? I need to talk to you.'

She drew back. It was incredible. Here was someone I loved more than anything in the world acting as though I stank. Resentment started to bubble within me.

'I was seeing one of the curators here about an exhibition. I never thought you'd sink to this! Not twenty-four hours after I'd gone!'

'Eh?'

'Only twenty-four hours!'

'Sue, what in hell are you talking about?'

Her teeth showed. 'I'm talking about you! Consoling yourself, I suppose you'd call it! I thought you might have seen some sense after I left. But no! What did you do? So predictable! My God, I suppose I should have known! You planned it, didn't you? You were pleased to be rid of me, were you? So you could be free to do what you wanted?'

'No, I wasn't. Look, I'm sorry about what's happened to Mitch Woods, but you can hardly call it my fault, can you?'

Her face showed puzzlement. 'Mitch Woods? What has Mitch Woods got to do with it?'

I frowned. 'Wasn't that what you were talking about?'

'No, I wasn't! I was talking about you, consoling yourself with that nubile nurse! Just your type, I suppose? I hadn't been gone for more than a day! Not a day! The whole world knows about your goings-on! Very cleverly arranged, I must say!'

88

'Hey, wait a minute, Sue! Hang on!'

The whole gallery was going quiet. An attendant in a dark uniform sidled closer, as though our exchange was a preliminary to an attack on one of the canvases. Some people were openly staring.

Sue dropped her voice. 'I certainly won't hang on! Don't deny that you took her out to dinner at a wildly expensive place! She's let the whole hospital know! And I have to put up with poor Gillian Roberts's sympathy! My God! You are an absolute bastard! I want nothing more to do with you!'

'Sue, you've got it all wrong. Honestly. I—'

I was talking to myself. She was walking out of the gallery, heading for the main entrance. I went after her, ignoring the startled visitors staring at me.

'Sue, for God's sake!' I caught her shoulder from behind but she wheeled like a tiger-cat, stopping short.

'Let go of me! Don't touch me!' Her eyes glared into mine. 'I'll scream for help!'

I stood back. Suddenly, I'd had enough of this. More than enough of it. This was degrading. I spoke calmly, keeping my voice low. 'Very well. If that's what you want. I'm damned if I'm going to explain how wrong you are.'

She stared at me. For a moment we stood facing each other. 'Go on,' I said. 'I wasn't following you and I won't follow you. So go on. Away with you. I'm not going to explain, now.'

Her face moved as though she was going to say something. Then she turned round and marched off through the revolving doors, out on to the pillared terrace into the fading, afternoon sunlight. I was left to the stares of the passing crowd, who soon lost interest.

Quite a day, really. Quite a day. The reliner's garages at Gunnersbury Park. A murdered restorer, Mitch Woods, at Kilburn. Hours with the police and another session with Brandon. Useless research at Leicester Square. Dim paintings in the National. A chance encounter with Sue and another bruising, damaging break with her, despite my best intentions and thoughts in the Library. Quite a day. Threats of arrest. Wonderful accusations. Sam Johnson assuming the worst with me and Kate Theaker. 'You haven't changed at all, have you?' Sue ditto, assuming the worst.

I had a pal in Ulster once, a chap who ran a pub. Everyone thought he was having an affair with the widow who ran the pub opposite, even though he wasn't. He was on his way to visit her one evening when the local policeman winked at him, broadly, as he passed. 'You may as well, John, for you're blamed with it,' the bobby grinned.

The National Gallery was emptying. People were going home.

You may as well, for you're blamed with it.

I got a taxi home, washed, changed and got into the Jaguar. As luck had it, I reached the hospital dead on seven. I parked in the most senior consultant's parking space in the forecourt, right opposite the entrance. The scruffy porter buzzed out, looked at the Jaguar, looked at me and buzzed back in again. At ten past seven nurses came scuttering out of the badly-fitting entrance doors and I half-leant, half-sat on the boot of the Jaguar, watching them. It was dark, now, but the entrance lights showed everyone clearly. Kate Theaker was the sixth one out.

She tripped lightly down the steps, saw me, slowed down and then walked across to me. I saw the other nurses glance at us as they went by. She was in her uniform but somehow looked a bit different. Somehow more optimistic and certainly a lot more friendly than the last time I'd been at the hospital.

'Hello,' she said, simply.

'Hello. How's Nobby?'

She nodded slightly. 'Holding on. Not talking. But holding on.'

'Great. Talking of talking, I have one or two things to tell you.'

'Oh?'

I smiled. 'It's a complicated story. I wondered if I could tell it to you over dinner?'

Her eyes went guarded. 'Dinner?'

'Yes, dinner. Out of London. It's quite good weather for October. There's a place on the river near Windsor. I

90

thought you might like a drive out of town. Get a bit of fresh air.' And tell the hospital about that, too, I thought.

She looked past me to the light-blue Jaguar sports car, crouched waiting in the parking space. 'Is that your car in our senior consultant's space?'

'Yes. It'll take no time in this.'

She licked her lips. 'Do I get time to change?'

'Of course! I'll run you to your flat first if you like. You'll be interested in what I have to tell you. There've been a lot of developments.'

'Windsor?'

'Near Windsor. On the river. We could go to the Compleat Angler at Marlow but the place I'm thinking of is a bit nearer. And quieter.'

She glanced round quickly at the hospital entrance. I half expected Redman to come out, but there was just the last nurse or two coming off duty. Autumn evening was settling into dark mistiness in a rather soft, dare I say it, impressionistic sort of way. The world looked less sharp. Kate Theaker walked round to the passenger door and let me hand her into the car. When we were both settled in and I was about to start the engine she caught my hand on the gear change lever. I saw that she was half-smiling in an affectionate sort of way at me.

'Tim,' she said, 'this is just for dinner? At Windsor?'

'Of course. Although, actually, when we've had our meal, we don't have to be cautious. Not if we don't want to.'

She shook her head sadly, looking at me across the car seat. 'Rugby,' she said. 'I look at you and I think of rugby football.'

'I do have some etchings. An etching. Of Dorelia, by Augustus John. Perhaps if you saw that, you could forget the rugby and think of me as a frightfully æsthetic, arty sort of fellow?'

'Etchings? See your etchings? God help me, how old do you think I am? Where are they, anyway? In your flat, I suppose?'

'Er, well, yes.'

She shook her head again, making the starched nurse's

91

cap creak very slightly and suggestively. The white apron over the striped uniform crumpled forward from her chest as she smiled, taking her hand off mine on the gear change.

'Don't get the wrong impression,' she said. 'I'm not going to make a habit of this sort of thing.'

CHAPTER 13

She wound the sheet carefully round her and sat up decorously to sip the mug of tea I'd given her.

'Tea in bed in the morning,' she said. 'What heaven. I haven't been served tea in bed for as long as I can remember.' She flashed me an amused glance. 'Do you serve all your lady friends morning tea after you've shown them your etching?'

'No—I mean—I don't have lady friends in quite the—profusion—that your question implies.'

She laughed. Her face looked good considering that early morning had just arrived. It was smoothed and somehow lifted, the skin lustrous and calm, the eyes humorous and inviting. Her mouth had lost the slightly downward trend I'd previously thought it was taking and seemed wider, more generous. She sipped the tea again and her lips were wet and warm as she spoke.

'No, I didn't think that.' She cocked her head to one side. 'I think that you're really quite a—a domestic sort of man.'

'Oh Christ. There goes my image.'

She smiled. 'Fancy yourself as a raver, do you? No, I don't think so. Domestic, I'd say. And the Dorelia etching is no great lure, I can tell you.' She looked round the bedroom carefully and her face went serious for a bit. 'Has she been gone long?'

'What? Has who been gone long?'

'Your lady friend. The schoolmistressy lady. She was in the ward with Mrs Roberts yesterday. Westerman? Sue Westerman?'

'Oh. Oh, her. Er, well—'

'No, I didn't think so.' She smiled. 'Don't worry. I'm not going to conduct an inquisition.' Her eyelids lowered for a moment and she looked at me speculatively from under them. 'I remembered you as such a thug. How old were you? In those old rugger days, I mean.'

I scratched my head. 'Oh, about twenty-one, twenty-two. Say up to twenty-five. I stopped then. Playing rugby, I mean.'

She nodded tho ightfully. 'You were a thug. I remember you as that. Ten years ago or so, was it? I was twenty then. And, my God, how innocent.'

'Ah. Well. I'm sure that experience has improved you. I remember you as a sort of rugger-bird in a head band and striped jerseys. You're much more alluring now.'

She grimaced. 'Flatterer. You won't get round me that way. But you, you're nothing like I imagined.' Her eyes came on to me and I noticed how full they were, blue and wide and serious. 'You're a long-term sort of man. Don't look so frightened! But you are, despite all the art and crime and things. You weren't like I'd—I'd expected. You're a kind and considerate man.' She looked down, quickly. 'I'm not speaking from a lot of experience in that way. But you are.'

This was embarrassing. I took a careful swallow of tea. 'Thanks,' was all I could say. 'But you have to take the responsibility, too. At least, fifty per cent of it.'

She smiled, but didn't reply.

'Actually, you've spoiled my image again. I fancied myself as a Latin type, you know, all macho aggression and the lady lucky to be the object of my passions. Lie back and think of England.'

She shook her head. 'Sorry. The age of feminism must have had an effect on you.' Her eyes were on mine again, seriously. 'She's very silly to be doing what she's doing.'

'What?'

'You're still in love with her, aren't you?'

'Er, well, in some ways, I suppose so.'

'In some ways?' She smiled. 'That's a typical masculine answer. 'In some ways. Do you like me?'

93

'Yes. Very much. I hadn't imagined you the way you are, either. The nursing disguise makes you look very severe. And you're not. You're a smashing girl.'

She put a hand on my own, sheet-covered knee. 'Thanks. You're making me feel much more appreciated than I was feeling before.'

'Ah. If it isn't *verboten*, may I ask if Dr Tony Redman *isn't* making you feel appreciated the way you should be?'

She crooked the corner of her mouth. 'You are on forbidden territory, really. But I had no illusions you were watching him. And me. No, he isn't doing me a lot of good, just now. Tony Redman is a shit, just now.'

'Oh dear. Has he ever married?'

She shook her head. 'No. That's his problem.'

'Really?'

'Oh yes. He's concentrated on his career for all these years and he's never had any trouble getting himself girl-friends. Now he's faced with decision time and that's what he can't take. So he's behaving badly.'

'Do you want me to punch him on the nose?'

She giggled. 'No, I don't. Although he deserves it.' Her face went serious again. 'If he found out about this, it would do much more damage than a punch on the nose.'

I shook my head. 'He won't. But a dose of jealousy will do his decision-making a load of good.'

'One way or the other.'

'If he's got any sense, there's only one way. I'll keep carefully in touch, I can tell you. Just in case.'

She smiled and put her tea down on the bedside table. One hand went through her hair to smooth it and I admired the bare arms, the well-shaped shoulders above the sheet, the bare back sloping down to disappear into the bedclothes. She turned to me and smiled again. 'You've done me a lot of good, Tim. What time is it?'

I looked at the clock on my bedside. 'Just gone seven.'

'Good God! I've got things to do before I have to go on duty again. I must go.'

She turned, but I caught her, wrapping my arm around the deliciously bare waist.

94

'Hey! What are you doing?'

With the free arm I took the edge of the sheet tucked across her chest and drew it down, right down, while she squirmed, until it was well below her knees.

'Just a minute, State Registered Nurse Theaker. Sister Kate. This patient needs a little more attention before you go.'

CHAPTER 14

'My dear Tim.' Jeremy was at his most avuncular. 'My very dear Tim. Things have come to a pretty pass, I must say.'

He couldn't do his usual hop, skip and jump down his office even if he had wanted to, because we weren't at his office. We were in a very good restaurant midway between the City and the West End, which I'm not going to tell you about because I want to get a table there unimpeded when I need it, and he wasn't agitated, which was making me rather worried. Normally, when the sort of events I have recounted take place, and I do regretfully have to confirm that they have a habit of taking place from time to time, Jeremy gets into a dreadful bate. Today, however, he was doing his avuncular, his man-of-the-world, his statesman-like, big broad flexible outlook act. It made me uneasy. The lunch had helped, of course. Mellowness was in the air. The empty bottle of claret had been removed. Port had accompanied the Stilton and memories of the Meursault served with the first course were happy ones. Coffee was on the table and Jeremy was casting regretful glances at his empty port glass.

'I suppose,' he murmured, 'in these austere times— austere dietetically, I mean—it would be considered extravagant to have a digestive brandy after one's lunch.'

'Oh, I don't think so, Jeremy. After all, we do have our health to consider.'

95

He gave me a reproachful look and ordered two extremely old and fine brandies. He was looking very well. Jeremy's height helps him to carry the odd stone or so of excess weight without difficulty or loss of grace and his blond hair has always given the impression that he is younger than his years. Yachting keeps his complexion of an outdoors hue and he's quite strong, from hauling in bowlines or docking the spinnaker or whatever it is they do when beating up and down the Channel in a stiff gale. Jeremy is riding his mid-forties in very good shape, the Bank starting to respond to his attacks on its tiller and his standing in the financial world gradually improving as he shifts his pennant from that of a freebooting privateer towards the respectability of the line.

I had had a very busy morning. After such a pleasant start, and having seen Kate Theaker safely back to her flat, I'd done a heap of work at the Bank, made an appointment to snare Jeremy for lunch and then I'd done Bond Street. Well, to be accurate, I'd done Bond Street and Cork Street and one or two other streets in beating about all the possible galleries that dealt in Impressionists, apart from Morris Goldsworth and Kennard & Crowe, who I'd already seen. I'd come up with a complete blank. Either I'd have to rely on Morris Goldsworth's private sources or I'd have to wait until something came up at auction, and that could be at the millennium or some date so far into the future as to be unimaginable.

'It's a pretty pass,' I agreed. 'The only whiff of a Monet or a Pissarro I've come across is at Kennard & Crowe. Their Pissarro might have been exactly what we wanted. None of the others referred to it, of course, trade etiquette, or more likely sheer jealousy, being what it is.'

Jeremy scowled. 'I don't blame them. I do not want to buy from Kennard & Crowe. I object to paying double the market price for a painting. It would be bad practice to buy from Kennard & Crowe.'

'I agree. But it goes to show. Perhaps the only source we'll come across will be someone like them, though.'

He shook his head vigorously. 'Never. Let us have no

defeatism. I know I can rely on you, Tim, to come up with the goods. You'll find something. Despite your magnetic influence where violence is concerned.'

'Oh, look here, Jeremy, that's not fair. I—'

'I know! I know!' He held up a hand. 'I withdraw the remark unreservedly. It wasn't your fault. Leads would have led the Force to this unfortunate man Woods anyway. I accept that.' He paused to take a sip of brandy. 'It wasn't about that—' a wave dismissed the Woods case— 'that my remark was made.'

'Oh?'

He swallowed. Then he took another sip of brandy. I waited patiently. Silence intensified into a puzzling but definite gloom. Jeremy appeared to be studying the table-cloth in front of him with rapt attention.

'Jeremy, if it isn't the Nobby thing, are we back to the Impressionists? I mean, I know it's disappointing for the moment, but as you say, one has had a certain degree of luck to supplement one's efforts in the past.'

He shook his head again. 'No, no. Sometimes I wonder, Tim, if you don't make a habit out of being deliberately obtuse.'

'Me? Why? What on earth are you talking about?'

He fiddled with his glass. A meaning stare was shot at me. Receiving a puzzled reflection, the stare dropped. He cleared his throat. 'Look here, Tim, we've known each other for a long time.'

'So we have.'

'So I hope you won't get upset if I mention something to you that is, um, perhaps something of a personal matter. We are both, as it were, men of this world.'

My eyes widened. There is no adequate response to a statement like that, so I waited.

'I mean, I know it's none of my business but we—Mary and me, that is—well, Mary's quite upset, you know.'

My eyes widened further. Jeremy's wife Mary, who used to work at the Bank, as Chairman's secretary, was a close friend in much the same way that Gillian Roberts was. Having married Jeremy and produced two offspring to add

97

to the White dynasty, she was slightly domesticated for the moment but still took a close interest in the Bank's affairs. In this aspect, with her previous knowledge, she was an invaluable help to Jeremy.

'Oh?'

'Yes. Well, I mean, she and Sue have always got on very well, you know.'

'Oh.' Grim understanding was beginning to dawn.

Jeremy shifted uncomfortably. 'I mean, I realize that thirty-five or so is a very difficult age, Tim. Very difficult indeed. I do realize that.'

'Eh? Thirty-five? Surely you mean forty-five, don't you?'

He bridled. 'Forty-five? Good heavens, no! One is one's prime at forty-five! One's prime!'

'Oh yeah?'

'Tim, really! Please let us not get sidetracked. Or descend to personal issues. I know how it is, you know. In one's mid-thirties one is constantly harassed by those who claim to remind one that one should have "made it" by now and all those childish things that used to be in vogue about careers. About City whizzkids being too old at thirty and all that rubbish. I can tell you, it's simply not true. Take it from me. And anyway, in your case, it simply isn't applicable. You have "made it" if anyone has.'

'What?'

'Of course you have. Look at your achievements. Look at the Art Fund. Look at your work for the Bank. Solid achievements.'

I stared at him in wonder. It might not occur to him, or be tactful for me as his assistant to point out, that riding shotgun guard to Jeremy and acting as player-manager to the Art Fund might not be considered by many to be the basis for a solid career in merchant banking.

'So you see, Tim, I can understand it if one gets restless at that age, but you've no need to.'

'Oh?'

'No.' He cleared his throat uncomfortably. 'And, I mean, the same applies in one's personal life. I mean, boys will be boys and all that, but there is a certain argument in favour of thinking in more settled terms, you know. At a certain point.'

I refrained from mentioning that he himself had not married until he was over forty years old. I merely raised my eyebrows politely.

He took another delicate sip of brandy. 'You mustn't think—I mean, this is very awkward for me, but I'm sure you know how upset Mary can get—you mustn't think that there's any spirit of *criticism* in what I'm saying, Tim, but is it not perhaps just a little precipitate, a shade hasty, to rupture what I'm sure has been a most happy association to, to, well, indulge in what is possibly just a passing fancy?'

'What?'

'After all, these things pass by very often, you must know that. As a man of the world. With your experience.'

I thought about the row with Sue that had caused her departure and this conversation to take place and frowned at him.

'I don't think that my friendship with Nobby is just a passing thing, damn it, Jeremy. I feel a responsibility to get to the bottom of what has happened to him, particularly in the light of his reaction in hospital.'

'No, no, no! I wasn't referring to that! You've quite misunderstood me. I wasn't referring to your disagreement about Nobby Roberts's case, although I realize that you may have used that as the, er, the trigger, so to speak, with which to set off your purpose.'

'My purpose?'

'Yes. Well, as I understand it. I may be wrong, of course, and am open to correction.'

'Jeremy, what in hell are you talking about?'

He sighed. 'Oh dear. This nurse is what I'm talking about. The nurse you apparently took a shine to when you and Sue visited Nobby Roberts in hospital. It's all very upsetting. I mean, we are men of the world, Tim, you and I, and one understands these things, but could you not have er, well, managed the thing without, um, without engineering Sue's departure from the premises quite so precipitately?'

For a moment the restaurant vanished. My mind went quite blank. Breathing stopped, blacking my vision. Surely my hearing was defective?

'I'm sure you must know, Tim, how fond Mary and I are of you and Sue. I mean, it's no business of mine and you can tell me to go to hell, of course. But Mary is really very worried. She doesn't really understand why Sue had to be evicted, so to speak, er, well, I'm sure there are other aspects, but so that you could er, well—'

My hearing wasn't defective. I was hearing correctly. It was incredible. There was no doubt about it. With a rush, feeling, coordination and fury returned.

'*WHAT?* You—you—think that I—you—Christ! I don't believe this!'

Conversation at adjoining tables had stopped. Jeremy looked about him, desperately. 'Tim! Really! Control yourself! You're causing an incident! Get a grip, man!'

My mouth was open. I held it like that until the maître d'hôtel heaved alongside, wringing his hands.

'Get me another brandy! Quick!'

He vanished like a ferret after rabbits. Conversation resumed slowly at the nearby tables. Jeremy was looking at me in alarm.

'Tim, you've gone quite *mottled*. Do you think another brandy is wise? Perhaps some fresh air—'

'Yes I do! Very wise! I need a brandy! Quick!'

'Tim, I'm sorry if—very awkward—I did tell Mary that —you wouldn't be—' He let his voice trail away. I noticed that he was really concerned. Somehow I managed to get control of my voice.

'Jeremy, have you been giving me the Dutch Uncle treatment because you think that I "took a shine" as you call it to "this nurse", as you call Kate Theaker, when we first visited Nobby? And that, as a result, I engineered a row with Sue to get her out? Is that the scene? Eh? I made the whole thing up so that I could—I could—'

Do what you eventually did, Tim.

Jeremy cleared his throat. 'Er, well, of course, no, well I'm sure that there is another view, so to speak, well, your view, but—'

'But Sue has told Mary that she left because I deliberately provoked her out of the place so that I could be free to have a go at a nurse I'd seen at Nobby's hospital?'

'Well. Not in so many words, no. I'm sure not. I mean, these things are always more complex than one imagines. Or seem so.'

'But that's the gist of it?' Brandies had arrived. I grabbed mine.

'Yes. Well, um, yes. In very broad terms, of course.'

'Jesus Christ.' I drank the brandy.

'Do be careful, Tim, I beseech you, please! Blood pressure, you know, can be a frightful thing! Lay a man out for good.'

'Blood pressure may be the very least of my problems. Blood pressure may be a welcome solution if this goes on.'

'Tim, Tim! Come now. I'm sure that with sympathy and understanding—'

'Stop! Stop right there!'

He stopped. I managed to get my breath back. With some difficulty, but back it came. I composed myself for the moment; dignity was essential, now. I marvelled at myself, although my voice sounded oddly thick.

'Thank you, Jeremy, for your kind solicitude. I much appreciate your concern. This can't have been easy for you and I shan't hold it against you. I realize that you and Mary have a heartfelt concern for us—Sue and me, I mean. You can tell her that I am not quite the shit that the story she has been given would indicate. Kindly assure her that the version of the facts you have been given is far, very far, from the truth. Nothing, in fact, could be farther. Further. Whatever. Sue has behaved execrably in trying to justify her appalling conduct. Thank you, very much for the excellent lunch. It has been memorable. I must say that it has been memorable.'

I managed to stand up. The restaurant rotated a little and then settled. Jeremy looked up in alarm.

'Where are you going?'

I got one foot out into the aisle between tables. 'I need some fresh air, Jeremy. Fresh air. I think that I shall go fishing.'

'Fishing? Fishing? Where on earth will you go fishing?'

'Up the reservoir, Jeremy. With a young friend of mine. Not, I should advise you, of the nursing profession.'

CHAPTER 15

It was very calm up at the reservoir. Young Jeff Woods sat on the grass just back from the concrete edge with his tins of maggots and other revolting aids to fish attraction around him. His rod and line were out over the water and his sinker bobbed cheerfully on the ripples raised by the light October breeze. The sun reflected off the sheet of water stretching to the west of us, somehow diminishing the forms and angles of other boys and men who sat behind their own tackle at intervals around the large expanse of water. To the south of us was a hazy panorama of North London: bumpy grey stock brick, slated gables and pottery chimneys interrupted by vertical factories or modern blocks, rusty gaps behind wire fences, stilted viaducts carrying distantly thunderous traffic. To the north, patches of green punctuated the undulating suburbs that disappeared towards an unimaginable rurality. The air hummed with muted sounds, some of them constant like the traffic, some instant and transient like near voice-calls or far, unexplained thuds. The effect was soporific, totally removed from the metropolis. I lay back on the grass and clasped my hands behind my head.

Prising the boy loose from his mother and attendant woman police constable had not been at all difficult. The WPC had been suspicious at first but Mrs Woods was tearfully grateful. Anything to get the boy out and about a bit, with reliable supervision of course, after the dreadful shock of his father's death. A ride in a Jaguar and a bit of fishing would be just the trick. The boy was calm, too calm; he sat doing nothing, not even reading. The WPC went outside to radio for permission; she didn't use the telephone in the Woods' frugal flat. I imagined her contact would be with the CID sergeant at the local police station, the one who'd started out hostile at my last meeting with Brandon, Sam Johnson, and the Drugs Squad man, Warren. I had concentrated on sucking a peppermint, not wanting to lose my licence for driving under the influence by breathing brandy fumes all over the WPC. Mrs Woods waited hopefully, tidying the boy up a bit, getting him to get his tackle together. I assumed that the WPC served the dual purpose of looking after the widow in her grief, for which WPCs have a justifiably superb reputation, and of acting as a guard in case the danger associated with the late Mitch Woods should spread to his widow and the boy. Evidently there hadn't been much checking to do when the WPC made her call because there were no objections. I was, it seemed, considered suitable enough to take the boy and be capable of handing off any opposition on my own. Perhaps they thought it would keep me out of trouble. The only condition was that he was to be home by six, which was imposed by Mrs Woods. She stuck a bar of chocolate into his pocket and watched him hop into the car with a brave smile.

The boy was quiet. He sat with his knees drawn up, watching the water, his eyes narrowed into the late afternoon sunlight. He wore a pair of jeans and a blue sweatshirt printed with a Tottenham Hotspur motif over a thick check shirt. They were the sort of clothes you could buy at the local Tesco's and so were his stained sneakers. He was an ordinary little boy of seven, the sort of boy you can see anywhere, rather pale from living in the city, rather thin, not from any lack of nourishment or deprivation but because boys like that are built like that, fishing boys who ride bicycles with rods strapped to the crossbar, tins of gentles in the saddlebag, hooks in their pockets. The thing that struck me when I put him in the car was how small boys of seven are. When he gravely shook hands with me, his hand had vanished into mine, thin and frail and crushable. He hardly came above my waist and his front teeth had only just grown back in. It seemed incredible; I couldn't remember being that small at that age, I couldn't remember being so defenceless and soft-boned yet shrewd and knowledgeable in a patchy, self-preservative sort of way. His eyes looked into mine with a depth that was disturbing, that saw something adults wouldn't see. It came home to me that boys of seven could easily be taken for tougher customers than they are and be damaged thoughtlessly by adults expecting them to have harder shells. I had therefore done up his safety-belt for him very carefully, feeling a bit self-conscious, as though he perhaps knew how to do it up himself and was tolerating my fuss with resignation, but then you never knew; boys of that age quite often can't do up their shoelaces, if they have any. What I had also forgotten was how boys of that age think of older boys, of young adults, of older men, what assumptions they make about them, which opinions are important to them. It disconcerted me a bit to see him look at me from time to time speculatively, as though I was something he wanted to make up his mind about.

He was obviously keen on fishing. I've never been a fisherman but I could understand it all as a hobby; the preoccupation with the kit, the type of rod, the bait, the quarry, the hierarchy of competition and the exciting advertisements in specialist magazines. All hobbies have the same features, whether for children or adults. I wondered whether his father had really liked fishing too, or whether he did it just to be with his child, to further a relationship hampered by the father's necessary isolation in his studio. Artists tend to be gregarious in their social habits to compensate for working alone, but the Mitch Woods I remembered had been a loner, a man with much to hide, who might like the peace and solitude and lack of query that being here, out in the open, might bring.

'Did your dad like fishing?' I asked the boy, more to open a conversation than to make a real inquiry. We'd been sitting in silence for what seemed like a long time.

He shook his head but didn't speak.

'He didn't? Well, I expect he liked to come up here with you all the same, didn't he?'

The boy nodded slowly. 'Yeah. But he didn't fish.'

'Just watched you?'

'Yeah.'

He glanced at me quickly and back to the water again. The sinker bobbed placidly. I wondered what sort of fish were allowed to live in a reservoir. I'd heard of some reservoirs where no natural life was permitted for purity reasons but then there were others with dinghy clubs sailing all over them. From the number of people fishing, this was a popular venue for the local angling fraternity, although I hadn't seen anyone actually catch anything. To angle hopefully was preferable to landing a fish, perhaps.

'Nice up here,' I said to the boy.

'Yeah.'

'Ever catch anything?'

'Yeah. 'Course I have.'

'Big?'

'Nah.' He held up his fingers, about six inches apart. ''Bout this size.'

'What kind of fish?'

'Carp. Tench.'

'No trout? No salmon?'

'Nah.' He shook his head, grinning. ''Course not. You've got to go to a river for them.' His grin told me he knew I was kidding.

'Yes. I suppose so. I was never much of a fisherman, myself. Used to catch sticklebacks in a jar from the local stream when I was little, but that's as far as I got.'

He nodded absently. There was a call from the far bank, where someone had landed something. I was caught off balance, trying to squint across the rippling water to see what the fish was when he spoke next.

'Why were you looking for me Dad? The other day?'

He was staring at me curiously, his pale face lighter than usual, drawn, concentrating.

'To talk to him. About a painting.' It hadn't been, of course, it had been about Nobby, but there was no point in complicating things.

'A painting?' His face was still taut.

105

'Yes. Your father was a fine restorer. He was an expert. He restored a painting for us, at the Bank, a while ago.'

The boy looked at me doubtfully, revealing some of that inner knowledge that children assume about their parents, about their habits and their failures which, seen from close domestic quarters, make it difficult for them to believe that the same parents could ever be anything too celebrated or admired.

'You work in a bank?'

'Yes.'

'Behind the counter?'

I smiled. 'No. Not behind the counter. I'm one of those people who works in an office, out of sight, doing something else. It's a bit like the art trade and your dad. The dealer out front in the gallery is like the clerk at the counter. Your dad was one of the experts behind, restoring the paintings, getting them ready for sale.'

His face was pale and set. His eyes had got bigger. 'You found my dad, didn't you?'

'Yes, Jeff, I did. Well, the police came at the same time as me.'

'Was it—was he—' He began to tremble. His face looked even whiter. 'Was—I mean was—'

I got one arm round his shoulders quickly as he crumpled and began to cry. With my other arm I caught the fishing rod he'd dropped and prevented it from sliding into the water. As he leant against me, shaking, I wormed my handkerchief out of my trousers pocket and gave it to him so that he could press it over his face. I was useless, helpless. Either his mother or the WPC should have been there but they weren't and I hadn't dealt with small, grief-shattered boys since I'd been at school. 'There,' I managed to say. 'Don't hold it back, Jeff. Let it come out.'

His voice, muffled in the handkerchief, was thick and clogged. It made noises that were hard to make out, although I could guess at some of them. I spoke as gently as I could.

'I know, Jeff. You're going to have to be very brave. To help your mother as much as you can. Try to think about

106

your father as he was here, when he came fishing with you. Do you remember? It helps to do that. That's what I did when they told me my father had died. He was a long way off when it happened and I was at boarding-school. So I know, you see, I know just a bit what it's like, although I was much older than you when it happened.'

No one seemed to take the slightest bit of notice as I held him. The peaceful scene and the distant lulling noises were completely unaffected by his grief. He sobbed into the handkerchief, quietening down after a while, returning to scale as a tiny figure in a huge, murmuring panorama. I slackened the arm I had put around him.

'You can keep the hankie. It's a big one and you'll find it useful.'

He nodded briefly as an agreement and thanks. He managed to raise his head a little and open his tearful eyes to look at his fishing-rod.

'If my dad hadn't had that telephone call it wouldn't have happened.'

'Maybe, Jeff. Maybe not. But you told the police about that call, didn't you?'

'Yes.' He sniffed and blew his nose.

'All about it?'

He nodded, head down again. 'I told them. But the police didn't like my dad.'

'Why not?'

A snuffle came as he wiped his face. 'He was in some trouble once. They gave him a load of aggro. I don't like the police.'

'I'm sure they didn't mean it, Jeff. They're only trying to do their best, you know.'

'I don't like them. They were nasty to him. You're not police, are you?'

'No, Jeff, I'm not. I told you, I work in a bank. But you did tell them, didn't you, about that call?'

'Yeah.' He shrugged his shoulders. 'He didn't say who he was. Just asked to speak to my dad. That's what I told them.'

'So you just passed the telephone to your father?'

'Yeah.'

'And then he went off to his studio?'

'Yeah.'

'And you told that to the police?'

'Yes, I did. Bloke didn't say his name.' He paused, waiting, waiting to release something that needed releasing and had done for days, something small and bottled and hard that set his pale face twisting with tearful anxiety.

I kept my arm round his shoulders. 'You recognized his voice, didn't you? You'd answered the phone to him before, hadn't you?'

He was still. I squeezed the shoulders gently. 'I'm not police, Jeff. If you tell me, I promise to bring you up here fishing again, soon. You should tell me, you know. I won't tell on you. Or get anyone into trouble who shouldn't. We'll come fishing together again if you'd like to. No one will hurt you, I promise.'

He looked up to stare at me fiercely, with tear-rimmed eyes.

'Promise?'

'I promise. We'll come back here soon.'

'In your car? The Jag?'

'In the Jag. I promise.'

He bit his lip. My handkerchief twisted tightly, wet in his hands. His voice was husky when he spoke. 'It was that bloke called Morris. Morris Goldsworth. That's who it was.'

CHAPTER 16

Bond Street was closed for the evening. By eight o'clock, that month, the sky was pitch dark. All the lights were on and most of the people had departed, leaving the street with the odd lategoer, hurrying off to a bus or train. Bond Street is a shopping street topped by offices; out of retail and office hours there's very little point in being there. I paced carefully up the pavement from where I'd left my car near Conduit Street.

I had stayed with Jeff Woods until the appointed hour and then run him home, stopping to phone Morris Goldsworth on the way. When we arrived at the Woods' the boy ran into his mother with relief and I could sense that she knew, the moment that she'd seen his face, that some sort of change had taken place. He wrapped his arms around her briefly and then handled his tackle into the back of the house saying he was hungry for his tea. She and the WPC faced me together expectantly.

'He's all right,' I'd said. 'He seems better. We had a bit of a talk up there and he asked me all about it. He's a brave little boy. I think it helped to get away for a bit. You know? It was nice up there, sunny and open. He obviously loves fishing.'

His mother nodded, smiling a little. 'He does love it. Thank you very much. I can see he's better. He hasn't asked for his tea since—since it happened. It was very kind of you.'

'Oh, nothing. The least I could do. I've promised to take him again.'

The WPC stared at me unflinchingly. Across her face various expressions of speculation, concentration, assessment, disbelief and careful consideration passed. Her eyes narrowed. Then she put on a bright look and thanked me with a brittle, cheerful formality that carried professional interest in my movements.

Very kind of you,' she'd echoed. 'Very kind indeed. The kettle's on; can we offer you a cup of tea? If Mrs Woods doesn't mind?'

I'd thought quickly about that. Mrs Woods obviously didn't mind. If I rushed off, the WPC would report back and assume I'd pumped the boy for something vital, something to be acted on very quickly. I smiled at her, easily.

'Why, that would be nice,' I said. 'Fishing is a chilly business and I'm thirsty. If it's no bother?'

'Of course not.'

The thirst was true. After the lunch with Jeremy it was a wonder that I hadn't got a major hangover, let alone a degree of dehydration. I didn't tell them the boy and I had

109

had a soft drink and an ice-cream; that was our secret and I knew he'd keep it. As long as he did full justice to his meal there'd be no problem and that is what he did. I drank tea and talked platitudes to the WPC and his mother while the boy ate, shooting glances of complicity at me from time to time. Mrs Woods lost a little of the tension in her face and began to fuss around him, buttering more bread for him and saying she wasn't sure how they'd be able to manage but she'd worry about that later. Mitch had left a little bit in the bank and there was always Social Assistance. She glanced at me several times as she said it, conveying something implicit, something she didn't want discussed, so I kept off the subject and said I'd come back to take the boy fishing soon, like I'd promised. Then I left for Bond Street.

The gallery was unlocked, as Morris said it would be. He came out of his back office, the one with the see-through mirror, as soon as I walked in through the door.

'Hello, Morris. Sorry to keep you late.'

He grunted. 'Doing me books anyway. Bloody VAT. Bloody special scheme. Here, let me lock up behind you. Bloody punters might start pouring in, buying paintings and upsetting our talk.' He grinned sarcastically. 'We mustn't allow that, must we?'

'Oh no. Who do they think they are?'

The gallery had a deserted air, like a suite of offices you visit at night when all the people have gone and the purpose of place has been abandoned. It made you wonder what all those paintings were there for with no one to look at them, what on earth all the fuss about art was, why bother. Passing down the right-hand row of them, half-seeing the coasts, the goose girls, the sunny fields where idealized harvesters cropped flawless stands of corn, I had a feeling of alienation, of dislike of the whole activity and its illusions. So what, I thought, so bloody what, there's so much of it and it's such a rat-heap, we all try to crawl one on top of the other, pretending we know more than we can possibly know. Artists are artisans, hard-working skilled men like any other craftsmen, who grin at all that baloney the writers dream up. I'm tired of it.

'You don't look very happy.' Morris Goldsworth gave me a quick-stepped, thick-lensed glance from his big aggressive spectacles, the glance shifting irritatingly from one focal field to another. 'What's the matter? Found a Keating and lost a Picasso?' He grinned at his own humour. 'Have a seat and tell me your life story.'

I sat down opposite his desk chair while he lowered himself into it. The Harold Harvey was on the wall to my right, another country scene in typical manner, except that it wasn't. I pointed to it as Morris Goldsworth looked at me looking.

'That Harold Harvey,' I said. 'It's really very good, isn't it?'

He frowned. 'What do you keep harping on about that bloody painting for? I'll have to take it down if you don't give over. I've told you; I was tucked up on it good and proper. Keep it as a lesson.'

'You haven't answered me, Morris.' I took out my wallet, removed a twenty-pound note from it and laid it on his office desk. 'There you are. Twenty pounds says it was painted by Mitch Woods.'

He didn't answer. The eyes behind the thick lenses were magnified like those of a fish, but they were expressionless as he looked down at the note. I put my wallet back in my jacket pocket, leaving the note where it was.

'They always said that the West End boys must have paid Mitch Woods to stop doing that sort of thing.' I kept my voice level. 'I expect you were one of the ones who paid him, weren't you, Morris?'

He bit his lip. For a moment he went on looking at the twenty-pound note and the account books and invoices strewn on his big pedestal desk. Then he nodded, briefly.

'You paid him off? You and a bunch of the others?'

He nodded again.

'After you bought that Harold Harvey or before?'

'After.' His voice, returning, was emphatic. 'Of course it was after.'

'So he kept his bargain?'

'Sure.' Goldsworth nodded positively. 'As far as I know. Or anyone else.' He grinned ruefully. 'You have no idea

111

how good he was.' He jerked his head at the painting on the wall. 'That was just for starters. Took me in a treat. Mind you, I didn't buy it from him direct. Through a dealer, that was. Mitch was dead cunning, really. Used to feed them through an auction here, a dealer there, an antique fair somewhere else. He spread them about. He was good. Different artists, all quite pricey but not too pricey, not so as to raise suspicions. A few thousand here, a few hundred there. Old canvases, usually relined, but not always. Clever stuff. Most wouldn't get away with it, but he had a knack for that period. Late nineteenth, early twentieth, Newlyn School, Camden Town Group, you name it. He was good, very good. The ageing technique was terrific. Most of them overdo it, but not Mitch Woods. He had it just right. Mitch was a bit of a joker, you know. He used to like the idea of cocking a snook at all of us, at getting away with a clever fake. Seeing how good—or bad—we were. A lot of fakers like that. For them, the thrill of fooling all the experts is more important than the money.' He scratched his chin and shook his head sadly. 'Mitch once built in a spot-the-deliberate-mistake into an Augustus John he did. It was a portrait of John's wife Ida, the Nettleship girl, painted in April 1906. The mistake was that she died in March that year, of course. The buyer was an expert on Augustus John but he never twigged till after he'd bought it.' Morris grinned savagely. 'Mitch enjoyed that.'

'Was he paid a lot? To quit, I mean.'

'Yes.'

'How much?'

Morris Goldsworth stroked his chin. 'How far is this going to go?'

'Nowhere. Nowhere beyond me.'

'Twenty-five thousand.'

'Twenty-five thousand?'

'Cash. *Cash.* Tax free. It'd take a man like Mitch a long time to save twenty-five thousand nicker after tax. Wouldn't it?'

'Oh sure. But it must have been well worth it to you lot.'

''Course it was. Some of us could have lost that ourselves

individually in no time, let alone a group. It was worth it, sure it was.'

'And he just packed up?'

'He did. Signed a secret affidavit we lodged in a vault.' He grinned. 'Would have been difficult to enforce legally but it was the psychology of the thing.'

'What happened after that?'

'He stopped. What d'you mean, what happened? What should happen?'

'I heard he got into trouble.'

A sad look came into Morris Goldsworth's face. 'I suppose it was the money. He couldn't handle it.'

'What about the boredom?'

The sad look remained as he nodded, flashing the thick lenses. 'I know. Going back to being an ordinary restorer, that was it. Anti-climax. No excitement. He blew it. First it was a bit of booze, then they said it was drugs. Coke and heroin, you name it; he went off the rails. I guess most of the money did, too.'

'But you knew about it? You were in touch?'

He shook his head vigorously. 'No, I wasn't! He cleared off. I lost touch completely. I just heard about him from time to time. Odd contacts and remarks. That was it. He was gone.'

'You never used him as a restorer?'

He shook his head again. 'No. Not again. Swear to God. I used him a lot in the old days, but not after that.'

I gave him my most direct look. 'You called him, Morris, the day he was murdered. On the phone. You went to see him at his studio. Before I arrived and found him. I must have just missed you.'

Silence. Morris Goldsworth stared at me, the glasses square-on this time, so that I could see his eyes very clearly. Then he licked his lips carefully as though they had gone very dry.

'No.' The voice was a whisper with no conviction, no truth behind it.

'I went fishing today, Morris. With a little boy called Jeff. He's under protection. The police and mine. Mine

113

particularly, now. He's only talked to me because his dad inculcated a mistrust of the police in him. So no one else has been involved. I've come straight to see you, so that there'll be no misunderstanding. You get me? No leaks from me or the boy. Not so far, anyway.'

His eyes dropped. Morris Goldsworth took the big tortoiseshell glasses off and wiped his face with his handkerchief the way he had on my last visit, showing the big bare defenceless expanse with its poor eyes that would only get a blur from the world they peered at. Morris was large, with too expansive a waist, a man whose aggression was, I now realized, bound up with fighting his way up from nowhere and with his size, which distanced him and made him seem threatening to others.

'He was dead.' It was louder, but still almost a whisper. 'He was dead when I got there. Lying on the floor. Turned me stomach over. Still does, when I think about it, when I can still see it. On the floor, face down, by the desk. Poor old Mitch.'

'He was already dead?'

'As a doornail.'

'So you didn't do anything? Didn't call anyone?'

'Like hell! What do you take me for? Eh?' The eyes came up, jerking boldly beind the tortoiseshells. 'Think I want my life buggered up by a load of nosy coppers? It was bad enough over Charlie Benson and I never had too much to do with him, not as much as I've had to do with Mitch in my day! Aggravation, they would have given me. Real aggravation. Not me, Mr Tim Banking Simpson, not me! I scarpered pretty damn quick, I can tell you. Sweating, I was. Never moved so smartly in my life.'

'You didn't touch anything? Move anything?'

''Course not! What would I want to touch anything for?'

I frowned. 'Well—that depends on what you were there for. What were you seeing him about?'

'How should I know?'

'Eh?'

'How should I know? He didn't tell me, did he? He phones the gallery up while I'm out, see, and Cathy takes the

114

message; will I phone him, important. Haven't heard from him for months. So I ring him up once I'm back and he says will I come over and see him, matter of some importance, can't talk about it on the phone. I hedged, I can tell you. I didn't want no trouble and I've heard he was in deep with some bad lads. The drugs, I mean. So I shilly-shallied, see? But he insists. Says he's sure it'll be worth my while. I'm the only one he trusts.'

'The only one he trusts? Why?'

'How should I know?' Morris Goldsworth made an odd expression, twisting his mouth into a dubious pucker. 'I've used him in the past, I agree. Paid him a fair price. Business, wasn't it? No use paying a good restorer badly, you'll lose him to some other bugger just when you've got him doing the work the way you want it. So fair's fair. When we came to paying him off, to stop him turning out those bloody fakes I mean, I said we had to make it worth his while. So maybe he thought I was a soft touch, I don't know. Anyway. Anyway.' He closed his eyes for a moment, pausing on the word as he repeated it solo, to give himself time. 'Anyway, I went. When I got there, there he was.' He shivered. 'Croaked on the sodding floor. That's all I need, I thought, that's all I need. Sod this for a game of marbles, I'm not getting the plod and spending days of my life explaining my restoration accounts to them while Mitch's drug-peddling friends stalk me down from queering some pitch I don't know sweet FA about. This has nothing to do with me. So I scarpered. I never thought that kid of his would know who I was. How the hell did he know, by the way? I'm sure I never gave my name when I called.'

'He's got a long memory. He remembered your voice from before.'

'Christ.'

I sat back in my chair. 'You've made it worse, Morris. From a police point of view, I mean. Much worse.'

'If they find out.' He gave me a long hard stare. 'If they find out.'

I pursed my lips, remembering my promise to Sam Johnson. 'What time were you there?'

115

'Dunno exactly. Half ten, maybe. Maybe a bit later.'

'I must have been there not long after you. I got there some time after eleven. So did the police. Don't misunderstand me, Morris, I believe you, of course I do, but this might be important to them. Something we don't know about could come out of this.'

He made an expression of part-disbelief, part-resignation. 'Something we don't know about? Then it's best left unknown about. I don't see that I can do anything about it. Mitch is dead. What good will dragging me into it do? Can't bring him back, can I?'

'Morris, for God's sake, the police are scouring that studio with fine-toothed combs and a feather duster. God knows what forensic evidence they'll come up with. You probably left a fingerprint or something of yourself there.'

'Not me, I didn't! I was bloody shocked but not too shocked to check I hadn't held the door handle without wiping it afterwards. I didn't touch anything inside.'

'It still won't wash. They're going to let nothing stop them. Look, Morris, I meant to tell you last time but I forgot, did you sign that recent petition from the West End dealers asking for the Art Fraud Squad to be reinstated? The one that said how all the art crime was increasing and they couldn't do without the old Squad that was disbanded in '84?'

'Yes. We all did. Why? What's that got to do with it?'

'What's that got to do with it? Nobby Roberts, who used to be in the Squad, was shot three days ago, down in Dulwich. He's in a coma. Keeps mumbling Mitch Woods's name. So the police are dead hot after Mitch Woods's killer with a vengeance because he's probably the same, or connected with, Nobby Roberts's attempted murderer. And —what's the matter?'

Morris Goldsworth's mouth had opened and his face had gone white, deadly white, with the glistening of a horrid cold sweat on his forehead. The opening mouth had interrupted me but no sound came out of it. The lips worked, moving slightly.

'Are you all right?'

116

'He was here.' The voice had got dry again, devoid of moisture as though the brow had drained the larynx to supply the perspiration it needed.

'What?'

'That mate of yours. Roberts.'

'Here?'

'Yes, here. In my gallery. A couple of days or so before you say they shot him. The Chief Plod himself. Asking me a lot of questions. Five days or so ago, it must have been.'

'Nobby?' My voice was incredulous. 'Nobby was here? In your gallery? What on earth did he want? Why didn't you tell me?'

'Because you never asked, did you? That's why! You asked about Pissarro, not the plod. It's not my business to keep track of everyone! He was asking about the trade generally. Who's who, and who does what and all that. The usual stuff.'

'What for?'

'How the hell should I know?' Morris's voice rose defensively. 'When do the plod ever tell you what for? What they're thinking? What they're at? Eh? When? You tell me.'

'For God's sake.' I put my head in my hands. I hadn't had time to talk to Morris about Nobby the last time. Here I was tearing about like a mad game dog on the trail of a mythical fallen bird and all the time Nobby Roberts's tracks were crossing mine or running parallel to them or echoing them. A vision of the bandaged figure in hospital came back to me. No wonder there'd been such a reaction from him, no wonder. Something he'd been chasing impinged directly on to the world in which I moved, something his unconscious senses told him there was a danger I might find or might be able to discern. The sound of my voice, penetrating that bandaged pumpkin, had set off nervous alarm bells that shrieked at him. I tried to imagine him, unharmed, standing in the gallery talking to Morris, the lean, keen athletic figure in its dark suit set against the bulk of the picture dealer in his thick goggles, a contrast like putting a greyhound next to a St Bernard. What in blazes had Nobby been after? Why

117

Morris? Why Mitch Woods? Why was he wandering around Dulwich?

'What sort of questions?' I almost glared at Morris now. 'What in hell did he want?'

'Oh, bloody hell.' Goldsworth threw up his arms in despair. 'All sorts. Mainly about who is in the business now and that sort of thing. Claimed he was getting out of touch, the old Art Squad being disbanded for so long. Who's still going and who isn't. That sort of thing. Picking my brains. You know. There's been so much new money coming into art. You know that. Lots of yuppies and inherited money setting up as dealers. Big backers. All that rubbish. Who's left of the old gang. Who the new boys are. Who's just a front man for a bank and who's still an owner-driver, like me.'

'Oho.' I remembered the Drugs Squad man, Warren, and his remarks about Nobby looking into—what was it? —cash flow aspects, banking and so forth. And Brandon, saying that artistic involvement was not relevant. 'Oho. I think I know what he was getting at. Or starting to get at. Or sniffing at an idea about.'

'What?' Goldsworth peered at me inquisitively.

'Money, Morris. Sources of money. I recollect, back in those Whistler days, being with Nobby and Sam Johnson at Chelsea nick after a particularly nasty incident. Nobby said that one exercise he'd done during his training days was a Fraud Squad investigation into the sources of finance of the major West End galleries. Very interesting, he said it was. I think he was probably updating that study.'

'Why?'

I put my finger on my nose. 'Hush-hush. Part of a secret investigation. My thoughts on that will have to be developed for a bit. But thank God you told me he'd been here; it opens up a whole new line of thought for me. Anything else he talked about?'

Morris shook his head. 'No. Not that I can remember. But look here—are you going to tell your rozzer friends about my being at Mitch's or not? That's what I want to know.'

118

I swallowed. 'I've promised to keep Sam Johnson fully informed. You don't want me to?'

He opened his mouth, closed it, then opened it again, looking at his desk. 'Bugger it all. I'll never get me VAT returns done now. If you promised, you promised. I didn't know that your pal Roberts was in this. I'll tell them. Tomorrow morning. All right?'

'All right.' I felt enormously relieved. 'Thanks, Morris. I'll not mention it to Sam Johnson until you've spilled your beans. OK? Tomorrow afternoon I'll chat to Sam. I want to nip into the Bank tomorrow morning to get something else under way. Is it a deal?'

He nodded and stood up. 'It's a deal.' Then he sighed heavily. 'Damn you, but I suppose it'll be a weight off my mind. Especially now.'

'OK.' I stood up as well. 'That's enough for one day.'

'I should say so.' He picked up some papers. 'I have to switch the lights off from in here. You go ahead and I'll follow you to unlock the door.'

'Right.'

I sauntered out into the back of the gallery as the banks of spotlights went out, darkening the place section by section in an eye-plunging blackness. It took several seconds for my vision to adjust itself. The rectangles of painting on the walls became blank tablets, subject-matter disappearing as only the dim light from the street kept the gallery visible from within. A large canvas on an easel in the window blocked off most of the outside and a poster on the glass door obscured the view across to a silversmiths opposite. Morris came out of the office, closing the door as he snapped the last light off.

'Clocking-off time at last,' he said. 'Thank heavens for that.'

Together we sauntered down the gallery, past the plein-air canvases that were invisible now. Morris started to unlock the front door, stepping ahead of me.

'Damn it.' I suddenly remembered. 'I left my twenty-quid note on your desk.'

I saw his teeth flash in a grin. 'Thought it was me tip.

119

Bankers like you don't bother about little things like a twenty, do they?'

'You bet we do. Especially when it's mine.' I turned and strode back towards the office door. 'And especially when I would have won the bet about the Harold Harvey.'

He chuckled as I heard him unlock the front door from the inside. I reached the office and went in without finding the light switch because I knew exactly where the twenty-note was.

'Sorry,' I heard Morris rumble to someone at the doorway. 'We're closed. We open at—'

There was a dull, flat crack like a half-thud, that cut him off. Then another one. Then a momentary silence. I jerked my head up from the pedestal desk, where I'd picked up my note, and peered through the one-way mirror that Morris used to survey the gallery from his office. Morris was standing just inside the doorway, holding his chest. Blocking the doorway, a man stood pointing at him and I could half-see a car drawn up at the kerb. Then there was another dull crack, more percussive this time, from the man's pointing finger. Morris let out a crying gasp as he buckled backwards to fall heavily on the floor. Then there was a silence again, except for the unmistakable diesel pinking of a taxi's engine somewhere up the street. The man lowered his finger, which I now saw was a pistol, and walked briskly into the gallery, heading for the office door.

I went down under Morris's pedestal desk and into the central well with a speed and silence that was remarkably supple for an older rugby forward. It was a large desk, generously-sized like Morris, and was hard up against the wall. I bunched myself tightly into the well, right back towards the wall on all fours, screwed up like a squirrel, and prayed.

The gunman was nervous. He peered quickly round the office, hardly stepping further than the door. The light went on briefly, then off again. I began to feel my blood pressure rising as I kept my breath held back, not making a sound. A silence continued as he seemed to wait, not doing anything, just standing there. I heard him tread softly back into

120

the gallery, going over to Cathy's desk. Then another silence for maybe five seconds. Then the door closed loudly, almost with a slam. I heard the keys turn in the lock from the outside, where the gunman must have reversed them from where Morris had opened up. A car engine revved up and a flicker of light indicated movement.

Silence fell upon the gallery again. I came out from under the desk, breathing still very quietly, moving very cautiously and silently. Crawling round the desk, I reached the office door to peer into the dark space lined with expressionless oblong shapes. The light from the street fell more distinctly at the front end of the room and it showed Morris's bulk quite clearly. His thick tortoiseshell spectacles had fallen off somewhere and his dead face had that big, bare, defenceless look that I'd noticed when he took them off himself, not much earlier.

CHAPTER 17

Vine Street Police Station is not a place best recommended for an evening in London. If you've ever cut through from Piccadilly to the Regent Street quadrant by using Swallow Street, where Martinez Spanish Restaurant used to be and where Veeraswamy's still serves a good curry, you'll have seen Vine Street on your right, hardly a street at all, just a dead end with a blank modern police station façade on the left-hand side. Vine Street Police Station used to figure cheerfully in jovial P. G. Wodehouse stories when young men from Oxford got done for trying to pinch policemen's helmets on Boat Race Night, but it isn't at all like that now, not with the drug addicts' problems all round Piccadilly Circus. It's a serious, blank, cheerless sort of place, lighted by pale neon tubes that make everyone look ill.

The interview room got quite crowded at times. Various people came and went. Sam Johnson arrived about an hour after I'd been in there and Warren, the Drugs Squad man, arrived shortly after him. Warren seemed to infer that if I hadn't actually done in Morris Goldsworth myself then I'd been responsible for it. What mostly seemed to nark him was that I'd got the information out of Jeff Woods in the first place, information that they hadn't been able to get, and then that I'd gone to see Morris before passing the information on to the police. In Warren's view that made me a sort of accomplice, one of the other side. He didn't like the way I couldn't describe the gunman, couldn't identify him.

I tried to be reasonable at first. I was still very shaky and upset. I tried to get Warren to see that it was perfectly fair for me to go and ask Morris for his version of the story before unleashing the hounds of the law on to him. I also pointed out that they had more information as a result of my talk to Morris than they would have had without it; Morris would have been dead without their knowing that he'd been to Mitch's that day. Warren didn't like that. He also didn't like the idea that I thought that Morris had probably been telling the truth. His tone was offensive and he implied that not only was Morris a chronic liar but that visits from me had a necrotic effect on people like Morris and Mitch Woods. That made me angry, which in retrospect was a healthy improvement on the condition I had been in, but it didn't help my relations with the police, especially Warren. We ended up shouting at each other, with Sam Johnson shutting us both up, acting as intermediary. The more I got involved with Sam the better I liked him. But there was a point, somewhere around midnight, when statements had been taken and sergeants and photofits had come and gone, when Sam Johnson, his own eyes puffy, bloodshot and black-ringed, gave me a strange, clairvoyant sort of look and said:

'You know, Tim, I've never really considered it before but, remembering some of the things you've been involved in, always honestly and with the best of intentions I'm sure, it seems that those around you would have been best off if you hadn't started the course at all. Nobby Roberts always said that you are a sort of magnet for corpses, especially if they were involved in the fine art trade. I used to laugh at that but now I'm coming to believe him. I think the best thing we can do is to follow you round and see if we can anticipate events rather than doing post-mortems on them. For the first time I can remember I'm not sure that Commander Brandon's instincts might not have been right. Sorry to say it, but it's starting to look that way. Isn't it?'

I didn't answer him. When you've just missed being murdered yourself, seen a long-standing art dealer dead on the floor murdered in cold blood, remember a good restorer's body lying congealed in his studio, and have the image of your closest friend wrapped in plaster and bandages hard in your mind, you tend to avoid suggestions of paranormal qualities in yourself. What you need is a strong drink and some sleep.

It was nearly two o'clock when I got home and could indulge in a lot of the first and a modicum of the second. It didn't come easily, the second, and I tossed and turned badly, waking up at six and then drifting irritably into a doze that seemed long but wasn't. In the end I gave it up and had a bath, which helped me to pull myself together and gave me an appetite for breakfast, which I found strange until I remembered that I hadn't eaten anything the night before. I found enough cereal and bread to fill up with and demolished the lot of it. The day didn't exactly look good, but it seemed a bit better.

I was stacking a breakfast mug and a plate into the sink when the doorbell rang. I look at my watch; just after eight o'clock. The weather had turned frosty by night and for the first time there was a faint rind of white on the morning twigs in Onslow Gardens outside. I hadn't noticed it much but the season had arrived when you start to dose your rooms with the occasional burst of central heating, just to keep the chill off. Another year was coming to an end.

The doorbell rang again.

I glanced quickly round as I put my jacket on. The place was quite neat and I was respectable, clean, shaven and tucked into my business suit. My head only throbbed mildly. I took a quick squint into the bedroom. I'd made the bed and there were no traces, at least none that I could see, of

Kate Theaker's visit of two nights ago, but you never know with a woman, what she'll find. From which you'll gather, at this time of stress, that I hoped my visitor would be Sue.

The doorbell rang again, peremptorily. Sue would have used her key. Or would she, given the present situation and her accusations? You never know with a woman.

I brushed some crumbs off the table by the window and hoped they wouldn't show on the carpet too much. My heart started to beat rapidly in anticipation. I strode across the room, summoned up my strength and, once into my diminutive lobby, swept the door open.

'Tim!'

She was well-built, middle-aged, strongly-featured. Her hair was permed into a rather solid grey helmet. Behind her, Gillian Roberts peered nervously over her shoulder.

'Good God!' I said, completely taken aback. 'Enid Westerman?'

'Tim!' The tone wasn't promising. It was accusatory and it rang thoroughly, without a quaver. 'Susan says that you are behaving abominably. I'm deeply disappointed.'

I gaped. Gillian Roberts made a frantic signal at me. I stepped aside and Enid Westerman swept past me into the flat. Gillian tripped along behind her, giving me a quick peck on the cheek. I grabbed her before she could get fully into the living-room.

'How's Nobby?'

'Oh, Tim! I think he's starting to come round!' Tears filled her eyes. 'I do believe he's going to be all right.' She gave me a clutch and another peck on the cheek. 'Thanks to you.'

'Oh no. You know Nobby. Indestructible. I—'

Enid Westerman had made an unmistakable reconnoitre of the bedroom, at least as good a reconnoitre as you can make by hopping about the right spots in the living-room and craning your neck in various directions. Then she started to scan the kitchenette.

'Is there anything,' I asked, with considerably pompous dignity for a man as weary as I suddenly felt, 'I can do to help, Enid? Can I offer you some coffee, perhaps?'

She stared at me, drawing herself up. I stared back. She looked around the empty flat, swallowed, and then sat down suddenly on a dining chair by the table.

'Oh dear,' she said. 'This is awful.'

'You haven't called her Susan since she was about eight years old,' I said reproachfully. 'I don't think I've ever heard you call Sue Susan before.'

'I hate London,' she replied mournfully. 'You know I never come here if I can avoid it.'

They say that if you want to know what a girl is going to look like when she's older, examine her mother. I reflected that if Sue got to look like her mother, things might not be half bad. She was a bit heavy but not too much, and she was still a very grand woman, handsome and splendid, like a vintage vehicle that has been lovingly maintained. The permed hair-helmet wasn't at all typical of her; she must have had it done to give her confidence, like girding up for battle.

'I'll get you some coffee,' I said. 'I suppose Sue has gone to work, has she?'

Gillian nodded and sat down, relief showing on her face, whether because I was alone in the flat or whether because Enid had crumpled somewhat from her aggressive start, I wasn't sure. I got them coffee and served it from a tray on the dining table.

'It's nice to see you, Enid,' I said, handing her the sugar. 'You're looking very well.'

She gave me a glance as she took two lumps. 'You can stop that,' she said. 'None of that. You won't worm your way around me, Tim Simpson.'

'Worm round you? Of course not. We know each other much too well for that, don't we? Tell me: did Sue send you or have you come here of your own accord?'

'There's no need to be unpleasant. No, Sue doesn't know we're here. We came because she went off to work early—some exhibition or another in Reading and we thought we'd take the chance of catching you before you left for the Bank.'

And find out if there was anyone else here, I thought wryly, so as to gain a strategic advantage. Perhaps it was

125

lucky that I'd been at Vine Street until so late an hour;
no, I couldn't ascribe any luck to the death of Morris
Goldsworth. I gave an involuntary shiver.

'We wanted to talk to you confidentially.'

'Ah. I see.'

She blinked at me. I smiled at her. 'Come on, Enid, cough
it up. What do you want me to say?'

'Oh, Tim!' It was a wail. 'What on earth is going on?
Why are you like this? I'm so upset. You know that you
and I have always got on so well. I mean, I've tried to
understand all this—' she waved a spoon around the room
—'I mean your living together and so on, though poor Basil
would never have approved, but I've tried to be modern
and so on, that's the way things seem to be nowadays and
Sue has always been adamant about it but now—now—'

'Now what?'

'Well, I'd hoped, I really had hoped, that eventually—
you know—you seemed to be so settled at last, and now
Sue says that you won't change, won't give an inch, and
from what she said I fully expected the place to be full of
sultry sluts of some sort and it's not, so I don't know what
to think now, I really don't.' She sipped her coffee. 'When
you smile at me like that it ruins all the things I was going
to say. You are awful, Tim. The trouble is that you and I
have always got on far too well, that's the problem. I want
you to be absolutely honest with me, now, please. What on
earth is going on? Sue says you're behaving disgracefully
and it just doesn't seem like you.'

I smiled again faintly. Her distress was so obvious. Enid
Westerman led a contented life down at Bath, secure in the
Englishness of herself and her friends. To her, London was
a foreign city, a den of iniquity where nothing went right
and virtually no activity could be approved of. I felt sorry
for her; on the whole it was starting to look as though she
was right.

'Enid, I'm sure you know that I have proposed marriage
to your daughter on more than one occasion and have been
turned down flat every time. There's no more that I can do.
I'm not going to risk humiliation again.'

126

'Oh, Tim! Oh really, my dear boy! I'm sure she doesn't mean it, you know.'

'Be that as it may. It so happens that I am doing something, a sort of investigation, of which Sue does not approve. I know that things have been a bit hairy in the past, so she has reason to be concerned. But this is exceptional. In this case—'

I broke off. In this case people were going down like ninepins and the wife of my closest friend was staring at me intensely, tears in her eyes, hands clasped, mouth opening.

'Tim!'

'Look, I'm sorry, Gilly, but—'

'No, Tim, listen! Listen to me! You've been terrific and you're a dear friend. But I hate this. Hate it. If I thought —and I know if Nobby thought—that he'd been the cause of you and Sue splitting up he'd—no, we'd—never forgive ourselves. Never. Please, Tim, please. I know how you feel. But this is a police matter. It's very serious. Can't you leave it alone? You know how Nobby would hate you to interfere. Sue is right. You shouldn't involve yourself. I feel terrible about it.'

'But that's just it, Gilly. I must involve myself. You saw Nobby's reaction to me at the hospital. You saw it yourself. There's something, isn't there, that I can help with? Something Nobby was doing or did in Dulwich that involved Mitch Woods and art and me or my knowledge in some way! It's not just that I want to bash whoever it was that did that to Nobby. It was to start with, I admit it, sheer bloody fury, but now it's something else, something that perhaps I could put my finger on. Something that I know or might know or could figure out given half a clue. There's no chance that I can stop now, you know that, especially after what's happened since.'

Gillian Roberts smiled a little before she answered. 'I had to try. But you and Nobby are so similar sometimes. I wish you weren't. You egg each other on. Tim, I've tried to explain to Sue, believe me, but she won't listen either. It's a sort of test case for her. A decision case, between her and another imbroglio. A choice. Perhaps you don't realize how

127

important it is for her. She wanted to be consulted, to be asked, but she could see that you were determined, that you wouldn't listen, wouldn't consider her. And then—well—and then there's been the other matter.'

'Other matter?'

'This nurse.' Enid Westerman's interjection was emphatic. 'This wretched nurse.'

'What nurse?'

'Oh, Tim, really! I'm a mature woman, you know! I've known many people. I'm not going to embarrass you or anything. But the wretched woman has been crowing all over the hospital. Now I want you to tell me quite honestly, Tim; this is just between us. What is going on between you and this other woman? I'm not going to make a scene or pass on things which are confidential but if I'm going to help I must know the truth. Is Sue right about this affair?'

'Of course not.'

'Well then: what is going on?'

'My dear Enid. You have my categoric assurance that I have not installed her in this flat. You can see that for yourself. I can also give you my word of honour that I did not manufacture a row with Sue so as to get her to leave and clear the decks for an affair, as you call it. It never occurred to me. I pleaded with Sue not to go but she was adamant. I met her accidentally at the National Gallery and tried to explain that the only way I could get any information about Nobby was via his nurse but she snapped me off short. I'm sorry she feels the way she does but I'm not going to be dictated to by a woman who refuses to marry me and still wants to eat her cake and have it. Freedom is freedom, I said to her, it works both ways and it still does. If she's free, then so am I.'

There was a silence. They gave each other unhappy stares. I knew what they wanted to say to me. They wanted to say that love has its obligations, with or without signed declarations and certificates, that logic has no part in emotion, that just because you can't impose a condition like marriage on someone you have no right to make counter-conditions. But they understood what I meant. They also understood that being reasonable and compromising and giving way doesn't win any contests and that love is a contest for much of the time. They were both married women.

Enid Westerman looked down into her coffee cup. 'Sue says that you took the nurse out for dinner.'

'I did. Of course I did. No one would let me near Nobby. No one. How would I have found out about Mitch Woods —about Nobby muttering his name, I mean—if I hadn't taken her out and asked her? Besides, she's in love with Dr Redman, not me, and he can't stand me at any price. So she's making him jealous by using me. Ask anyone at the hospital. They'll confirm it to you. I'd have done anything to find out what happened to Nobby and she was my only chance. I've got no excuses to make.'

Enid Westerman said nothing. Suddenly she looked very sad. Gillian Roberts was biting her lip. A thought occurred to me and I got up to look out of the window. Down on the pavement below, two unmistakable plain clothes policemen loitered near my door. Gillian was still being guarded, I was relieved to note. Or were they there for my benefit? I took Enid Westerman's hand.

'Look, Enid, I'm sorry about all this, really I am. And I really appreciate your coming to see me all the way from Bath. When all this is over perhaps we'll all see it differently. But I can't stop now. Can't you see that?'

She sighed. 'Of course I understand, Tim. Basil—Sue's father—was a mild man but when it came to principles he was immovable. So I understand. But I wish I didn't. I wish you wouldn't. I wish—no, it's no good wishing.' She put her cup on the table. 'I must say that everything looks very neat and tidy. Apart from those crumbs on the carpet. Actually, another woman would have been easier to cope with. Come on, Gillian, we'd better get to the hospital and see what progress has been made.'

Gillian Roberts nodded and smiled. She stood up and came across to kiss me gently on the cheek. 'Please be careful, Tim. Nobby may soon be well enough to talk. Try to wait for that. Will you?'

129

'I'll try.' I didn't make it sound very convincing.

She shook her head. 'I didn't think I could persuade you.'

At the door Enid Westerman kissed my cheek formally as well. Her eyes held mine as she said goodbye. When they were through the door and half way down the stairs the two of them stopped to look back at me intently, as though to memorize what I looked like. As though they didn't expect to see me again.

CHAPTER 18

The frost had been harder out at Gunnersbury Park, where less heat from city buildings was available to dispel the night temperature. A weak autumn sun had melted the cold white crust off most objects and buildings but here and there the deep shadow beside the railway viaduct still glinted white along a hard line which the sun was moving steadily backwards. The rusting chain-link fence had drops of moisture beaded on to the grimy wire mesh between the concrete posts, where the line of lock-up garages stood coldly functional behind their sealed steel doors. The single entrance to the reliner's, cut into one of them, was locked by a large padlock on a hasp. I knocked, but no one answered.

I sat on the boot of the Jaguar and stared at the scene. It was ten o'clock. Under a nearby railway arch two young mechanics were taking the back axle off a redundant yellow ex-Telecom van. The toy distributor's men were loading large cardboard cartons into a brown Luton. A smell of spray cellulose paint hung in the outside air but the temperature was still fresh and the sun wasn't warming my back much. It was very unusual. The reliner was a precise man, professional, who was always at work by nine-thirty at the latest. He tended to work late, when things were quiet and everyone else had gone home, but although he didn't start early, nine-thirty was usually the latest.

The door was padlocked, on a hasp.

If I'd been a smoker I'd have lit a cigarette. I searched

my pockets for something like a mint or a sweet but that was hopeless. I hadn't bought anything like that since Sue left. She liked strong mints and occasionally a bag of marshmallows, which tasted like polystyrene dusted with icing sugar to me; I like plain chocolate.

'Come for a respray, squire?' It was the paint-spattered lad I'd seen drinking a mug of tea on my last visit. A huge wedge-shaped cap of ancient Scottish ancestry covered his head and thin stovepipe jeans clad his limbs like leggings. He looked like something out of an old shipyard photograph as he grinned at me.

'No, thanks. Not yet.' I grinned back at him.

'Nice motor.' He gestured at the Jaguar. 'Be nice to do one of them some day. We get the saloons here, older ones, but not the XJSs. Not here in this lot, anyway.

'Oh.' I gesticulated at the reliner's door. 'Seen them this morning?'

'No. Not yet.'

'Unusual, isn't it? He's usually here by now.'

'Yeah. Although, wait a minute.' His face changed. 'There's his barrer, over there.'

'His—oh, his barrow. Car. I see. You mean the white Granada estate?'

'Yeah. Over there.'

A white Granada estate car stood near the chain-link fence, parked beyond the end of the garage block.

'You sure?'

'Yeah. That's his. Must be here, mustn't he? Don't live here, do he?'

I walked back to the padlocked door and hammered on it with my fist. Silence. Grit on the asphalt road crunched under my shoes. I hammered again. Nothing. A welder across the way, where cars stood waiting their turn for treatment, tipped his welding mask up over his head to stare at me. The wedge-capped boy shrugged.

I trudged past the garages in the increasing sunlight to where the white Granada stood cold on the asphalt. Condensation had run down all over it, down from the roof to streak the windows in thick stripes of moisture, droplets

131

hanging everywhere, even on the windscreen where the wipers had made no arcs of difference. A faint touch of frost still wet-powdered one small patch on the shaded boot.

The car had been out all night.

It made me step backwards quickly. That car had been out all night. A rapid tingling made even my fingers curl in anticipation and apprehension. I gave an involuntary glance towards the silent line of garages. Beyond them the welder was still watching me and the paint-sprayed lad was still standing near the padlocked door. This wasn't right. Maybe the reliner had gone home some other way, in another car, the previous night.

Why wasn't he here, then? It was quarter past ten, now. He couldn't be collecting canvases up in the West End because the Granada, with its wide rear door, was what he would use for that. He was a secretive man; I had no idea where he lived.

I marched back towards the lad. 'Telephone?' I asked him. 'Anyone got a telephone I can use round here?'

He jerked his thumb towards the railway arches. 'In the office. Mind you, he's dead mean with it.'

'I'll pay him.'

A pound coin waved under the manager's nose got the use of the phone. I wasn't in luck. Sam Johnson wasn't at his desk at wherever the number he'd given me should have located him. They said they'd pass the message on. I gave them the address and said it was urgent. Then I emerged into the increasing sunshine, butterflies fluttering in my stomach. The welder had put his helmet back into position and was creating showers of sparks close to a heap of car parts. The wedge-capped lad was fiddling with a paint spray-gun, but shooting glances in my direction from time to time. I went back to my car and sat on the boot for what seemed like the duration.

It was nearly an hour before a dark red Ford Sierra came crunching carefully down past the viaduct. It stopped close to me and Sam Johnson got out of the driver's seat. From the other side the Drugs Squad man, Warren, got out and stared at me without enthusiasm before they walked up close to me and stood for a moment without speaking.

'Hello, Sam,' I said. 'We must stop meeting like this.'

He didn't smile. 'I've guaranteed Jim Warren here,' he said, 'that you wouldn't waste our time. I told him: Tim Simpson wouldn't call for us, urgent, for nothing or without good reason. We aren't sitting about waiting for fun most of the day. He knows that, I said. Especially after last night. This'll be serious.'

'Follow me,' I said.

We trudged across the asphalt to the line of garages and up to the door where the padlock mocked us. The wedge-capped boy put down his spray-gun and stared.

'What's this?' Warren demanded.

'This is a reliner's.'

'A what?'

'A reliner's. A reliner is a man who relines canvases for the fine art restoration trade. Most canvases need relining after a relatively short time, sooner than people think. The major galleries like the Tate and the National employ their own reliners. The trade use a commercial reliner with vacuum tables. That is what goes on inside here.'

They looked at me without speaking.

'This reliner gave me Mitch Woods's address,' I said, talking directly to Sam. 'I went to Mitch's from here the day he was killed. When I met you. Remember my statement at Kilburn? This reliner does work for Mitch, or used to when he was alive. I came here to ask him what work he'd done for Mitch recently, in the last two or three months. It's a hunch I've had, you see. I've been here since ten, but no one answers.'

Warren frowned. 'So what's the problem?'

'The problem is that he isn't here. Nor is his wife. He's always here, he or his wife or the lad they employ. They never leave it unattended except at night.' I gesticulated towards the Granada estate. 'That's his car. It's been here all night. All night, you understand me? All night?'

Warren still frowned. 'Have you got his home address?'

'No, I haven't. But that's his car. I don't think he's at

133

home.' I looked at the padlock. 'I don't like this. Something's wrong.'

Sam Johnson looked at me carefully, without changing his neutral expression for a while. Then he addressed the padlock. 'That's not a snap padlock. That's a heavy, multi-lever job. You can't just snap that shut and go. You have to have a key and lock it, deliberately.' His gaze left it and went away towards the Ford Granada. 'You have to step outside and lock this.'

'Unless,' Warren said, sharply now, 'someone locks it for you.'

'Or doesn't,' Sam Johnson said, peering intently at the padlock. 'Unless someone pushes it shut to make it look as though it's locked. Like wedging the hoop in with a bit of cardboard, for instance?'

Warren looked at him, looked at the padlock, and made a small, indeterminate sound. Sam Johnson took a handkerchief from his trouser pocket, folded it once carefully and took the padlock gingerly in a grip protected by most of the handkerchief. With a spare corner of material he pulled gently on the thick steel hoop that passed through the hasp. A tiny piece of card fluttered to the ground as he lifted the padlock clear.

'Well, well,' Warren said. 'Fancy that. Not very security-minded, your reliner, is he?'

'Very. Very, very, very.'

Sam Johnson put the padlock down on the asphalt carefully. Then he used his handkerchief to seize the hasp and pull the door open.

'Hello?' he called cheerfully, putting his head into the doorway. 'Is there anybody ho—'

They were hard men, Warren particularly. The Drugs Squad are not selected for squeamish stomachs. But the cry Sam Johnson gave as he and Warren went through the doorway was echoed by Warren and stayed in my ears long afterwards. It had a strangulated horror in its tone, horror and shock blended with a nausea that soon communicated itself to me.

The boy in the white coat who I'd seen cleaning canvases

had had the most merciful death. He lay, still in his white coat, behind one of the big vacuum tables where they had shot him, clean and quick. The reliner was tied to a chair with his back to me and I couldn't see his dead face. His wife had been tied spreadeagled over a table. Whatever they had been doing to her before they killed her had made the reliner twist and writhe and heave in his chair so that the cords cut into his clothes like garrotter's wires. His position was unnatural, distorted, like a broken doll's when it is strapped carelessly into a child's high chair. Over in one corner a filing cabinet had been pulled open and its contents, papers and files and hundreds of photographs, were spilled all over the floor. There were Instamatics and 35 mm slides mixed with invoices and reels of dark negatives, prints scattered with copies of letters and receipts. It was a huge heap of material, spilled and mangled and strewn violently, as though a mad gorilla had searched for a peanut in a haystack of paper. A smell of burnt glue hit my nostrils.

I managed to get back through the door before I started to heave. I leant with one arm up against the steel doors as I vomited up first the coffee I'd had with Enid Westerman and Gillian Roberts that morning, then my breakfast, then deeper and deeper and more painful things that hurt like hell to bring up, acid things that wanted to go through my nostrils in horrid chunks while Warren sprinted to the Sierra to use the radio-telephone and the wedge-capped lad stared at me in horrified speculation and the welder took off his helmet to hurry over to the open door where Sam Johnson emerged and warned him back in a voice that was savagely unlike Sam. Then I became too giddy and ill to notice much. It seemed a long time before I found that I was sitting sideways in the open door of a police car and that there were vehicles with blue lights flashing on them and other darker vehicles parked about. Someone must have supported me across to the police car and sat me, half in and half out, like this, in the fresh air. Leaning over me, now, were Warren and Sam Johnson, propping themselves on the door jamb with straightened arms.

'What?' Warren was demanding. 'What the hell were they after? What did they want?'

'I don't know! I wish to God I did.'

'Well, then. What were you after? What did you come here for?'

'I told you. I came to ask the reliner if he'd done anything for Mitch recently. Just a hunch, that's all.'

'What hunch?'

'I really don't know! I thought that if he could tell me, I might get some clue to what this is all about. Why Mitch was murdered. Why Nobby was disturbed about him. Things like that.'

'What clue?'

'How the hell should I know? You don't know what a clue is until you fall over it, do you?'

'Three people have been murdered in there. A woman tortured for some reason. Think! What could the murderers have been looking for? What were they after?'

'I don't know. For Christ's sake! If it hadn't been for me they'd still be undiscovered. You're the ones with all the expertise and the forensic battery. You find out!'

Warren moved back slightly then, putting his hands down from the door-frame of the car. 'I'm sorry. I'm as badly shocked as you are, but you have to see my general direction. First you find Mitch Woods, then you're with Goldsworth when he is murdered, now you find this. So far the only thing connecting Chief Inspector Roberts, Mitch Woods, Goldsworth and this is you. I have to try and establish what else can link them. What the hell you think connects them.'

Sam Johnson cleared his throat. 'I have to say that we appreciate, Tim, that you called us as soon as you did. When you felt that something was wrong. You did the right thing and we appreciate it. You kept your word and you've had a terrible shock. Don't think we don't realize that.'

I noticed that Warren was looking at Sam Johnson intently as he said this, as though he didn't give a damn about the sort of niceties that Sam was enunciating, but Warren had at least apologized for his aggression and I supposed I had to be grateful for that. Sam gave him a warning look before speaking again.

'What else did the boy tell you, Tim?'

I blinked at him. The scene in the reliners had shocked everything beforehand into an amnesiac cloud. 'Boy?'

'When you took young Jeff woods fishing yesterday. Something else come out of that, did it?'

I might have known, I thought dully, I might have known they'd still be jealous about that. I couldn't have been so ingenuous as to think that they wouldn't wait for the moment to pounce on that again. Perhaps they thought there were further seams to be mined from Jeff Woods, seams the little boy would keep hidden from them.

'Tim?'

I swallowed. A vision of Morris Goldsworth's eyes, bare and defenceless, with their spectacles off, came to me.

'We know Jeff Woods wouldn't talk to us or that WPC, though she's good. His dad taught him to mistrust us. He told you about Morris Goldsworth, though. The WPC says he was a changed boy when you brought him back. Load off his mind? What else was there?'

I swallowed again. 'Just Morris Goldsworth,' I said, sadly.

'Sure?'

'Sure, just poor old Morris. That telephone call Mitch got was from Morris. When Morris got there Mitch was already dead. I told you last night a dozen times. And Morris didn't know what Mitch wanted.'

'Sure?'

'Sure.'

Warren stuck his face close to mine. 'You didn't think to tell us about your hunch last night, though, did you? The hunch that brought you here the next day, all on your own?'

'For God's sake! I thought about it afterwards! When I was at home. Where in hell have you been?' I gestured at Sam. 'You weren't at your desk this morning, were you?

137

How could I have talked to you about it? I had to leave a message for you when I got here, saying this was urgent, to get any contact at all. Even then it took you an hour to get here. Don't say I didn't play the game this time.'

Sam Johnson gave me a dubious look, then nodded. 'All right. We can give you the benefit of the doubt, I suppose, though I have some reservations. So our dead friend Morris may have had something to answer for too, perhaps? I expect he used this reliner too, did he? Is that what you think?'

I nodded weakly. 'I expect he did.'

Warren's face was still close to mine. 'Any other little snippets you think we should have?'

I shook my head. 'I told you about Nobby Roberts.'

'What about him?'

'Like I told you last night; about two days before he got shot he went to see Morris Goldsworth.'

'Well?' Warren sounded irritable again. 'What about it?'

'I don't really know. Morris said he asked about general things. I was going to ask the reliner something like that, too. To see if I could follow Nobby's reasoning. The reliner knew the West End trade backwards; he might have had a hint for Nobby, too. I thought you'd know all about it. Surely, you're the ones who know what Nobby was after. Aren't you?'

Warren didn't answer. Sam just stared at me. It was then that I realized, with a great bounding blow to the nerves, that they didn't. Know what Nobby was after, I mean. They didn't know what Nobby was after.

They didn't know what Nobby was after.

He must have been following a hunch on his own. In true Nobby style, while behaving logically and rationally and with all due discipline, Nobby had gone off on a line of his own, pursuing a line of his own. And he hadn't made it to the next briefing meeting because someone had shot him, tried to slaughter him first, along the A213 Selhurst Road not too far from his home on the edge of Dulwich.

No wonder Sam and Warren were distraught. No wonder they wanted to hear my every thought. No wonder they were hardly enamoured of Commander Brandon, shooing me off like that at the hospital. No wonder.

The only real pity was that I didn't know what Nobby was after, either. That was going to require a lot more thought on my part, a racking of brains for every clue that I could think of. The blood started to course back into my veins; now I had every reason to get back into the hunt, every justification I needed. Warren and Sam Johnson hadn't said as much but one thing was clear: I stood as good a chance of finding what lay behind all this as they did.

They let me go at around four o'clock after I'd made another statement. Sam Johnson had left by then but his face, looking at mine, was a picture of speculation. Warren said, eventually, that I should be electronically tabbed to make it easy for them to follow me, like one of those American prisoners. Sam didn't even smile. He said that it would take time to sift through the reliner's premises and his home, which they had located. If they needed assistance they would contact me. I was not to go anywhere far away and certainly not to take any initiatives on my own. According to Warren, Commander Brandon had advised them to fix me up in solitary confinement in a dungeon in the Tower of London until the case was solved. But I was elated, almost jubilant. Not having time to spend in the Library, I went to Hatchard's bookshop on Piccadilly instead, getting there just before they shut for the day. I find that research helps to get horrid images out of my mind. It seemed to me, then, that I dearly needed Sue to help me but, things being the way they were, I'd have to fend for myself.

CHAPTER 19

Jeremy White sat quite still behind his desk in the panelled office where he and Geoffrey Price and I had met to discuss the Art Fund's business so few days earlier. The large mahogany table we had used shone coldly in the window-light although the heating had come on now, with the onset of chillier weather.

'My God,' Jeremy said quietly, soberly and most unostentatiously for once. 'How absolutely frightful. Ghastly.' His eyes, watching me, were sympathetic. 'Dreadful. Is there any news of Nobby Roberts?'

'Encouraging. Not off intensive care treatment yet and not conscious in terms of talking coherently but showing very encouraging signs. It could be any day now. Before he surfaces, I mean. Gillian is looking much better.'

'Thank God there's some encouraging news from somewhere. Tim, you know you look absolutely washed out. Should you be at work?'

It was the following day. Events at the reliner's, which I had recounted to Jeremy, still had a fresh, horrifying reality lying sharp on the edge of my brain. I had spent much of the night reading. Now here I was, sitting in Jeremy's office, being told that I looked washed out. The morning light had not brought much joy. I had a headache. The news about Nobby might be better but if you considered Mitch Woods, Morris Goldsworth, the reliner's massacre, Enid Westerman and her daughter, the chance of finding what this was about, who Nobby's assailants were, the situation of Jeff Woods and his mother, progress with acquisitions for the Art Fund and a distinct lack of sleep for two successive nights, there wasn't much to celebrate. Nothing much at all. The only cause for satisfaction was that at least I hadn't had to see Commander Brandon throughout the latest events and that I thought I knew as much as the police did; something I was sure they wouldn't like to admit.

'You should take the day off,' Jeremy said, kindly. 'Go home and get some rest, Tim. You look shocked.'

'No,' I said. 'At least, not yet. I want to ask you a favour.'

'Me? A favour? Fire away—what is it?'

'I want to use some research department time.'

His face changed, brightening with interest. 'Our research department here? What for?'

'You remember when we first met for the Art Fund

review? When we agreed about the Monet and the Pissarro? You asked me about Nobby then. Remember?'

'Of course I do.'

'You said to let you know if you could help in any way.'

'I did. I meant it.'

'I'd like—' I fished in my pocket—'I'd like our research people to establish a full range of ownership—the whole chain—for these galleries.'

I handed him the list. Jeremy scanned it and then looked up at me sharply. 'You've started with Morris Goldsworth. You think—I mean—'

'I don't know, Jeremy. I'm not thinking. Not until I see the facts. One of the things Nobby Roberts was—is—good on is, or was, the ownership of some key West End galleries. I've no doubt that the police are now doing the same thing but I reckon I can save time by concentrating on a likely short list. They'll have to cast their nets wider, although I bet Morris is at the top of their list too. The other thing is that since the police disbanded the Art Fraud Squad their info may not come as quickly as ours. Because we're deep into art investment and because we collaborate with Christerby's we've kept our database pretty well updated. On all potential purchasers and galleries, I mean. It may take a bit of time for our research boys and girls to give me that info but I'll bet it won't take as long as the police. We'll have to use our sources in the tax havens to trace any new changes in ownership but they're pretty good. Pretty quick, I mean. You can charge my Art Fund budget with the cost.'

Jeremy smiled. 'I'm sure the Art Fund can justify the cost,' he murmured. 'It's just a question of priorities. Don't worry: I'll get a priority put on this. You should have it within a day or two.'

'Thanks, Jeremy. Thanks a lot.'

He put the list on his desktop. 'Good. Now will you go home until this information comes through? And, Tim: about Sue. I'm sorry that our lunch turned out the way it did. If there's anything Mary and I can do to—'

The telephone rang, mercifully cutting him off. He picked it up with an expression of irritation. 'Yes? Oh, I see.' He

141

looked up at me. 'Yes, he's here.' A hand went over the receiver. 'There's a woman to see you. A Mrs Woods?'

'Here? At the Bank?'

'Here. She says it's urgent, apparently.' Jeremy looked at me curiously, keeping his hand over the mouthpiece. 'Mitch Woods's widow? Would that be her?'

'That's the only Mrs Woods I know.'

'What do you want to do?'

I stood up. 'Tell them I'm going to my office. Ask them to show her up there.' My headache began to recede. 'She's supposed to be under police protection. What on earth could this be about?'

Jeremy spread his hands before giving instructions on the phone. I nipped along the corridors to my much less imposing office at the back of the building with considerable speed. There was just time to clear away some papers before Mrs Woods was ushered in, clutching a thin but sizeable portfolio case. I came out from behind my desk looking to see if she had an escort, but there was none.

'Mrs Woods? This is a surprise. Alone? What can I do for you?'

She held the folio case tightly to her in both hands. Her face looked drawn but defiant. 'Jill Chambers—that's the policewoman—took Jeff to a friend's to play. She's nice. There was a bloke stayed to look after me but he got a call and had to go to his car for ten minutes. It's been my first chance. I left quickly. I got this—' she indicated the folio case with a nod of her head— 'out from under the bed and came straight down here with it. First chance I've had.'

'Take a seat, Mrs Woods. Would you like some coffee?'

She sat down slowly, holding the case, which was about two feet by three, carefully. Coffee was brought and she relaxed a little, putting the case down to take up her cup.

'I heard what happened yesterday,' she said, her eyes on mine. 'I decided then to come as soon as I could.'

'At the reliner's? Did you? How did you know?' The news had not generally been released as far as I knew; the police wanted time before announcing the full extent of the affair.

'I heard the policeman telling Jill Chambers.'

'Oh.' I wondered how well she'd known the reliner and his wife. Probably not very well but some sort of nodding acquaintanceship could be expected. I remembered that the reliner's wife had mentioned Jeff being seven years old now.

'I was thinking of going to Morris Goldsworth but I can't do that now, can I?' She made a frightened gesture. 'I never did trust him but I'd never wish that on anyone.'

'No. But I don't think—'

'I trust you. And your Bank.' She interrupted me quite sharply. 'I couldn't tell you about it when you brought Jeff back the other day. You never can tell with the police. Mitch bought this fair and square but they might cause complications. And it's the valuation, you see. You can't trust hardly anyone about that, certainly not Morris Goldsworth. Mitch was much too trusting there. But I trust you.'

'Mrs Woods, I'm afraid I'm not following you, exactly.'

She put her coffee down. 'You've been very kind. I—I don't quite know how to begin. I'm alone now and I have to trust someone.' Her face set a little, becoming more determined. 'I'm going to trust you. I've made that decision, so now you've got me, I'm afraid. You're lumbered with me. Mitch was a very difficult man in many ways. Artists are, you know. He wasn't dishonest, not really, it was more like, like a challenge for him. Painting, I mean. He had a sense of humour, Mitch did, it was a lark to him, a lot of it. That came from working so much on his own, I suppose. He needed something to bring him back to reality, you see.'

'He was a brilliant restorer, Mrs Woods. All the trade respected that.'

'Well, I don't know. I'm his wife, so I saw him differently, I suppose. Recently he wouldn't tell me what he was doing.' She bit her lip. 'He wouldn't allow anyone in the studio. I haven't been in for months. The police know more about what's in there than I do. Well, you know the kind of trouble he had. A while back. I tried to stop him, to help him. You see, with Mitch it was always the getting away with it, fooling the trade, that's what he loved. He just didn't seem to have anything to live for after they paid him off; he went to pieces. Then recently he seemed better, much more cheerful, but he locked the studio himself. Wouldn't allow anyone in.'

I leant forward. 'Better? He seemed better? In what way, Mrs Woods?'

'Oh, you know, just more cheerful. Happier. He—he still didn't stop taking those things he'd been on, pills mostly, but he seemed to get out and about more. That's how he bought that lot.' She pointed at the portfolio.

'That lot?'

'Yes.' She hesitated. 'He bought it fair and square. In a market near the Portobello, as a job lot. I've got an invoice for it. It's all right; he bought it fair and square. But you never can tell these days, what they might say. They take things off you, you know.'

I looked at the case. 'Was this ever in the studio, Mrs Woods?'

'Oh no! He never took this to the studio. He was very excited when he brought it home. He said that if this was what he thought it was it would be our pension. It was like he was drunk. He made me hide it under the bed at home. I thought he'd been out on the booze or speed or one of those. He was flushed and feverish. I tried to calm him down but he was in a state. Then later I heard him trying to get in touch with that, that Morris Goldsworth.' She pronounced the name with distaste. 'I heard him. I never did trust Morris Goldsworth. But he was out, or away. I didn't know he'd called back until the other day.' Her eyes held mine for a moment. 'Jeff took the call and handed it to Mitch. I didn't know who it was. He used to get calls like that now and again and he'd have to go off. I asked him about them but he wouldn't tell me what they were about. Jeff told me it was Morris after he'd been fishing with you.'

'Mrs Woods—how long ago did he buy this portfolio? Recently?'

'Oh, not long ago—about maybe ten days or so. He was very busy, he said, but he still used to tour the markets looking for things. He said he'd deal with this when he'd finished his current job—some customer was leaning on him to finish something quick.'

'So he needn't necessarily have been calling Morris Goldsworth up about this?'

She looked dubious. 'Not necessarily. But I thought he was. I had a quick look though, you see, and there's some very good drawings in there. New and old. And canvases. With Mitch being what he was, I'm no good at sorting out what's right and what's dodgy. You know how he was; he had all those art books in his studio, everything, so he could check on the facts and produce the right styles, you know, and look up things like the dates and that. Lives of artists, he used to buy. What do you call them, bio something?'

'Biographies, Mrs Woods.' Biographies. Why have a biography of Conan Doyle among all those art books? Was Mitch a fan of Holmes, like Nobby?

'So I never did know what was what, never. When I saw these, and he was excited, I could tell—'

'You brought them to me? To be looked at here?'

She nodded vigorously. 'Yes. I know I can trust you. These are not safe under my bed. I want you to lock them up here at the Bank. And sell them for me if you're not interested in buying them for your Fund. Mitch told me all about your Fund. Will you?'

'Can I see them first?'

'Of course.' She picked up the portfolio and put it on my desk. It was a typical imitation leather, flat thin case about two feet by three, with a zip all the way round three sides, the sort of folio case you see in Covent Garden where ad men and graphic designers hurry on their way to presentations. She unzipped it all the way round. I held up my hand.

'Just a minute. Let me make sure you're quite clear on this, Mrs Woods. If you leave this here we'll give you a detailed receipt for it, properly signed. If there's anything we'd like to buy for the Art Fund we'll make you an offer which you can have checked by a valuer if you want. Otherwise we'll suggest you sell the items at auction and we have an association with Christerby's who will duly suggest a suitable selling price, but you don't have to accept their ideas if you don't want to. If you have an invoice there's no difficulty about proving your title unless the goods were stolen, which I'm sure they weren't if Mitch bought them fair and square.'

'Oh yes. I know I can trust you, Mr Simpson.' She opened the case wide. 'It was just a job lot. No one will claim them.'

Inside the case was a pile of drawings among which I could see two canvases, cut off their stretchers and pressed flat between drawing papers or thick card mounts in which some of the drawings were contained. I raised by eyebrows. 'Mitch bought this as a job lot?'

'Oh yes. The whole batch together.'

Nothing unusual in that. Job lots of drawings, or canvases, are often bought by the trade and broken up to isolate the valuable items. The rest can be chucked away or shoved into a jumble sale. This appeared to be a typical lot. I looked at the top drawing, which was an undistinguished sketch of a meadow with trees, unsigned, worth a few quid and no more. People accumulate things like these in drawers, I thought, my word they don't half squirrel things away, the trade have to leaf through hundreds of bits like these to find any ore amongst the tailings, what a life.

The second sketch was much better, though; a view of Carcassonne by Lamorna Birch, a bit faint but nice nevertheless, a couple of hundred of anyone's money. The third sketch was a bird, unsigned, and the fourth, in a mount, was a print of a dabchick or a moorhen, running like a turkey, by Detmold. No pension so far. Mrs Woods watched me anxiously.

The first canvas, pressed reasonably flat but with one corner dogeared over like the page of a mistreated book, was of a horse, quite a nice horse in a stable, not too primitive but typical of those simple nineteenth-century horse portraits with a dog in the corner and a hen advancing cautiously towards the grain on the floor. The horse leered at you out of one eye. Done up a bit, relined, put on a stretcher, somewhere between one and two thousand pounds. Useful, but still not a pension.

146

The second canvas was tight behind it, almost sticking to it because the paint was thicker. It was quite dirty and was a foreshore scene of mudflats with a fishing-boat beached on them and some other boats dotted about. Oh hell, I thought, another fishing-boat, there's thousands of them, remember Morris's stock?

'What do you think?' Mrs Woods couldn't restrain herself any more.

'Well—' I was about to make some mollifying remark when I noticed that there were houses along the right-hand side, perched along a jetty of some sort. Then I saw that there were buildings on the left-hand side as well. I wasn't looking at a foreshore at all, I was looking at a river, a tidal river with the tide out, rather like one of those Wapping scenes of Whistler's in which a tangle of shipping elaborated a river bend. But this was much simpler, less complicated, the boats less detailed and the technique more modern, more concerned with light and shade than precise effects, more, more, well,—

More Impressionistic.

Into my mind's eye there came the black and white plate at the back of Wildenstein's *Biographie et Catalogue Raisonnée*, the beached boats near the houses below, what was it, the Pool of London, where the ships came up the tide, back in the nineteenth century. And as I thought of it I snapped the angle light on my desk so that the powerful beam would rest on the dark dirty corner of the painting, where the tangled mud and foreshore brushwork half-embraced, half-covered the signature that the artist had boldly stroked on to the impasto for which he was celebrated. It was hard to make out and I had to spit on my hand and wipe the moisture across the corner before I could be sure of what it said but there it was, quite unmistakable despite the dirt, staring at me:

Claude Monet.

CHAPTER 20

Brondesbury and Gunnersbury Parks; Kilburn, Bond Street, Dulwich; the City of London, Onslow Gardens, Vine Street. My taxi took me to none of these but my imagination pictured them all as we sped along the Embankment from Blackfriars towards Westminster. Somewhere past the Savoy I got a glimpse of the Houses of Parliament in almost the way Monet might have seen them, grey and cold in a chilly autumn light. This was a strange London saga, one which appealed to my historical and biographical senses of the city, in which somehow all the odd, random pieces of art-historic information I stored away in the back recesses of my brain ought to have helped to produce a pattern, a picture that made sense. They didn't. There were too many disparate pieces, there was too much dissonance. I knew that this thing was about drugs and about art. Probably about laundering money. I knew that it was possibly about fakes or faking in some way. I knew that the criminals were ruthless, horrible, invisible. I had no lead on them.

My heart was pounding like a hammer, not from fear or fury but with sheer exaltation as the taxi swept past Parliament Square and out along Millbank. I clutched the portfolio case to me and pictured the scene to come in a few moments. I knew, somehow I knew, that this was a jackpot, this was it, the Monet was no fake, it was going to be lucky, a talisman, it would pull the whole unfortunate sequence of events back straight again. The taxi swept past the main stairway and round the side where I directed the driver. I leapt out, lavished a tip on him and crossed the pavement, clutching the folio case. I needed help; I had no desire to fend for myself any more.

The commissionaire on the staff entrance to the Tate Gallery looked up sharply as I came in the side door and then softened his face into a smile.

'Hello, Mr Simpson! Haven't seen you for a while. How are you?'

'Hello, George. I'm fine. Haven't missed Herself, have I? Still in, is she?'

'Miss Westerman? Oh yes, she's here.' He peered at the folio case I still clutched. 'What's that? The Mona Lisa?'

I grinned. 'No such luck. Want to look in?'

He nodded. 'I better had. Security regulations. Record the contents. I'll give you a visitor's badge, too.'

The folio case still had two drawings in it, neatly making a protective sandwich round the canvas. George nodded cheerfully and zipped the case back up again before giving me a pass. The rest of the case's contents were still at the Bank, where I had given Mrs Woods a receipt and told her that I thought that the canvas was potentially very valuable but that I needed an expert to check it. She went off happily, excited in a way that must have been inspired by my own enthusiasm. Naturally, I'd said, this was an entirely confidential matter between us and no one else would know the course or origin. She nodded brightly and I saw her to the door of the Bank, where she slipped off into the crowd, heading back for Kilburn.

The basement of the Tate Gallery contains various departments, offices, storerooms and other facilities. Sue Westerman was usually to be found in a sort of warren at the back, where corridors zigzagged among boxlike partitions. With mounting nervousness but joyful determination I marched along the corridors until I reached her door, where I knocked once and sailed in, almost running slap up against Charles Massenaux as I bounded across the threshold.

'Good God! Tim?'

'Charles?' I gaped at him, taken aback.

On the other side of a desk sat Sue, looking neat and well-dressed as usual. It did me a power of good to see her. I smiled happily at her perplexed and increasingly compressed expression.

'I'm sorry. Hope I haven't intruded?'

'Yes, you have.' Her first words weren't promising. She

looked terrific, though; it gave me palpitations just to see her.

'Oh, it's all right, you know.' Charles's tone was mollifying. 'I was just going. I'll, er, I'll let myself out.'

'No, don't go.' Sue and I spoke in chorus, causing Charles to jerk sharply, like a marionette. Then we both stopped, eyeing each other. She emanated a coldness towards me which was now noticeable, like feeling that perhaps you should have donned thermal underwear before coming into her exclusion zone.

'Look.' Charles was at his smoothest. 'I'm sure I'm going to be a little, er, *de trop*, if I may say so. You two have matters to discuss. I'll just—'

'No!' I put the folio case on Sue's desk. 'I'd be obliged to have your opinion, Charles. This is a happy coincidence, as it happens. I can't think of any two people I would rather have together at this moment. The two particular experts whose opinions in this field I most value.' I began to unzip the case. 'One an academic expert on the Impressionists and the other a commercial expert. What better could I have?'

I pulled the Monet out of its case and put it on the desktop, under their noses, feeling rather like an experimental conjuror. It looked much less impressive there in that light, rather dirty and simple and unremarkable, so that my forced cheerfulness, the brisk exterior manner I'd assumed over my internal condition, began to dissolve. A long, low whistle from Charles Massenaux helped to restore a lot of the façade, though Sue had said nothing. Her eyes were fixed down on the canvas.

'Good God, Tim.' Charles, for once, was awestruck. His voice had totally changed. 'How do you do it? How in hell do you do it?'

'Do you think it's kosher? A real one?'

'It looks like it to me.' He raised his eyes to Sue. 'What do you think, Sue?'

She licked her lips. 'I—I'm not sure. I'm still looking.' Her eyes were still down.

I couldn't wait any more. 'It's nearly identical to the one

in Wildenstein's book. *Boats in the Pool of London,* I mean. But I know; it should be tested.' I looked brightly from one to the other.

Charles Massenaux shook his head. 'Not too tested, I hope.' He picked up the canvas to peer at it, held it to the light, drew his finger over part of the surface. 'My first guess is that it's OK.' He put it back under Sue's nose. 'Sue?'

'Value, if it is?' I couldn't wait to hear what she'd say; the tension was getting to me.

Charles grinned. 'What percentage do we get for a valuation?'

'None.'

'Then I'm not saying. I don't suppose you'll sell it anyway, will you?'

'Not if it's genuine, no. The Fund will buy it. But we might recommend that you do an independent valuation for a fee.' Why the hell didn't Sue speak?

'Ah. In that case, I shall pronounce when called upon to do so. But my congratulations, Tim, congratulations. I don't know where you found it, but I must say I never believed you'd do it, never. Have you got a Pissarro, as well?'

'Not yet.'

'Give it time, eh?' He beamed at me. 'Give the boy time.'

'The boy is right.' Sue's voice was even; much too calm, too controlled, for comfort. I knew that voice well. 'Just like a little boy. Look at him. He's won the prize, so now he runs home with it held aloft, to await the adulation. Just like a little boy. Hoping that winning the school prize will blot out all other problems.'

There was a silence. Charles cleared his throat, looking down at the canvas, avoiding our eyes.

'I was hoping—' I kept my own voice as calm and as even as possible—'that I could obtain an independent and expert opinion on whether this is a genuine Monet. I appreciate that it may take a little time, but—'

'Oh, I think it's probably a Monet.' Her voice cut me short. 'It needs cleaning by an expert and of course it needs to be relined and put on to a stretcher, but it has all the things necessary to make it worth while spending time and money to check it out. I can recognize that. If it is right it's one of those he painted when he was over here during the Franco-Prussian War of 1870 to 1871. The Pool of London ones. You don't have to quote Wildenstein at me, of all people. You might at least have the decency to credit me with a minimum of knowledge in this field.'

'I didn't imply that you hadn't. Got a minimum of knowledge, I mean.'

'I suppose you think that this makes everything all right again, do you? It's pathetic, really it is.'

'I think I'll be off.' Charles Massenaux started to move. 'In fact, I know I'll be off.'

'No, Charles! Tim interrupted us quite inconsiderately, barging in here as though he owned the place. It's typical of him.'

'Off, Sue. I'm off. Sorry.' Charles slid round the door like a smooth serpent, giving me a faint wink as he went. 'See you both sometime. Sorry.' Then he was gone, leaving Sue and me to stare at each other.

Her glare seemed much fiercer than mine. I started to speak and then decided not to. Long seconds passed. 'Pity,' she said, after an age. 'Charles and I were just starting to have a civilized conversation. Then you came in.'

'Oh, really? Getting quite chummy with Charles, are you?'

She looked at me pitilessly. 'He came to make a gallant attempt to persuade me that you really were after Nobby's attackers and nothing else. The boys closing ranks, I suppose. Once we'd dealt with that, we actually started to talk about intelligent things for a change.'

'He was right.' Well, I thought, he was right. As far as he knew, anyway.

'And that makes it all hunky-dory, does it?' Her voice rose. 'You can go off and behave how you like regardless of what I think, and that is still all right? You can ignore my feelings and it's still all right? Never mind about that nurse, that's just an incidental insult, you can discount that because it's really just good old Tim Simpson laying the girls while he's off like a Mountie to get his man.' She gesticulated at the Monet. 'Then you can rush in here, throw that on the desk and I'm supposed to be so excited that I'll forgive everything and drop my knickers on the spot! Is that it?'

I stared at the Monet on the desk. I hadn't even stopped to tell Jeremy about it, let alone the police. I hadn't waited a second after Mrs Woods had left. I'd picked the thing up, wild with excitement, and rushed over to show it to Sue. Her big thing was the Impressionists; she'd never rated anything else as highly as them. I thought that if it was a real one, she'd be as excited as I was.

'Well?'

I picked up the Monet, if that was what it was, and put it carefully back into the folio case. There were other places I could go to try and get it authenticated. It looked a pretty dull painting now, but if it was OK, Mrs Woods would be funded for life and young Jeff could have any chances that money could buy. It wasn't a madly important Monet, it wasn't like one of the Giverny paintings or *The Houses of Parliament* or the *Grenouillère* or the *Terrace à Saint Adresse* but if it was a Monet, a genuine Monet, it would be worth high into six figures or, more likely, seven figures the way the market is now and that would make Mrs Woods a millionaire widow. Mitch must have known what he had got hold of, or at least suspected it, so why hadn't he done something about it? And was this what everyone was after, what Nobby had been attacked for, what Mitch and Morris and the reliner and his wife and the assistant boy had all been murdered for?

'Well?' Sue's tone had changed. I zipped up the folio case and picked it up. Then I turned towards the door.

I bit my lip. No, it couldn't be this. Who knew about it, except Mitch and his wife and maybe Jeff?

Maybe Jeff?

Or maybe Morris Goldsworth, who'd said that Mitch wouldn't tell him the reason for a meeting, but maybe he had.

'*Tim?*' She sounded concerned now, curious, as though the last thing she'd expected was for me to pick the bloody

153

painting up in a sort of defeat, put it away, and leave, feeling as lousy as anyone who has his moment of glory turned to ashes, his ace trumped. But she'd gone too far; I wasn't going to argue or plead.

'Where are you going? Answer me!'

The commanding tone broke my resolve. 'All right. I'll answer you. You left of your own accord, before I'd even spoken to "that nurse" and you made ultimatums you knew I wouldn't accept. You know that. You've told Mary White a lot of lies to justify what you did. I'd forgive you all of that because I think your lies were admission that you were wrong. I needed your help today and I came here to get it. I didn't stop to think, I just came because it was instinctive. You were right about my being just a boy; it has been lucky for you that I was. Was, you hear? Was.'

I wrenched the door open. I'd delivered as good an exit line as I could muster.

'Tim? Where are you going?'

But I was leaving by then, trudging back down the corridors where the other denizens, behind their partitioned boxlike walls, had all doubtless had an enjoyable earful of how not to effect a reconciliation. On how to behave like an eager, stupid boy, in fact. Sophistication comes late to some people.

And painfully.

CHAPTER 21

'Oh dear.' Kate Theaker sipped her tea thoughtfully. 'Oh dear, oh dear. So that's what it was all about.'

'All what was about?

'Last night.' She smoothed the sheet carefully over her nubile figure. 'All that fire and tempest and frenzied energy. All that vigorous action. Before you slept like a log.'

'I thought you said I was a kind and considerate man.'

'I did. And you are. Mostly. I'm not complaining, you know. I didn't say that there was anything to complain about.' She cocked an eyebrow at me and smiled in lascivious complicity. 'I didn't say I didn't like the occasional fire and storm and brutal passion. A girl sometimes feels flattered that she can raise such a riot. Sometimes. Although on this occasion there were other, should I say, compelling factors?'

Her thick skin was smooth and fair in the morning light, glinting under the curling locks that the night had dislodged. Her eyes regarded me steadily and fondly, with just a hint of amusement in them. 'Her loss was my gain, wasn't it? Your irreconcilable, prissy Miss Westerman?'

'Oh? Um, well. I don't know.'

Her smile broadened. 'We're good for each other, Tim. It's ironic, you know. Because neither of us is too—too involved, you know, too desperately anxious about the other, we can relax and enjoy each other. It so happens that I needed you last night as much as you needed me. I'd made up my mind never to see you again. And then Tony and I had a blazing row. Just before you called. And off I went, swept away in your flashy car to dine, not giving a damn about anything and liking you for what you are, not for what I want you to be or what I think you should be or for behaving how I think you should behave. Just for what you are. That means, of course, that neither of us is really dead serious about the other, doesn't it? Sorry, I hope that doesn't upset you?'

'No,' I said, thinking about it. 'I don't think it upsets me. And you've done me an enormous amount of good, too.'

'That's great.' She sipped her tea again. 'It has been wonderful to have a hideaway like this. To have been waited on and flattered and to have been desired the way you so obviously wanted me. It has been great.'

'Good.' I felt uneasy about her use of the past tense, but decided to ignore it. 'Er, if it isn't a forbidden subject, what did you and Tony Redman have such a row about?'

'Oh—' she pouted—'this and that. Especially that. He wanted me to sleep with him.'

'And you wouldn't.' I made it a statement, not a question.

155

'Of course not. If I sleep with Tony, I'm finished. I'd just be another in his long line of conquests. An available divorcee who succumbed. Doctors have it dead easy with women, you know, Tim. All that curing and knowledge of physiognomy gives them a head start. Quite apart from the professional respectability and the money, which isn't half bad these days. Women like experience, you see. Men, most men anyway, like innocence. Odd old world, isn't it? Women wanting experienced men and men wanting inexperienced women. I suppose that was the trouble with that clot Bruno, really. He was young and gauche and naïve. Much too simple for me.'

'Shame. I would have thought that old Bungo would have settled down to become a pretty experienced doctor-wallah, given time.'

'Given time, yes. About a century, I should think. I don't want to talk about Bruno, Tim.'

'Sorry.' I put down my tea and stared out of the bedroom window at the wet gardens outside, thinking of Sue and Sue's mother, and Gillian Roberts, and Nobby and dead bodies. Closing my eyes for a moment, I thought of Mitch Woods, who was the secret to everything and about whom I knew so little. Then I opened my eyes and saw Kate Theaker, fair and ripe like a full peach, smiling at my apology, with her blue eyes starting to get a faraway expression that told me that she, too, was thinking elsewhere and that this was it, an approaching terminal.

She took a look around the room. 'What time is it?'

'Coming up for seven.'

'Oh dear.' She put her tea down. 'I've got a committee meeting this morning. I'm on the staff-patient relations committee. It's a hell of a bore. But I'll have to go.'

I turned towards her. 'I can sympathize. I have to suffer a lot of committees. And minor board meetings, which are just like committees. There is one thing; a sort of compensation.'

'What's that?'

I got one arm around her and ignored her more vigorous struggles and squeals of half-angry protest until the sheet was well and truly removed and she was firmly in my grasp, half under me.

'As one committee member to another, Kate, there's a certain motion I'm going to put to you.'

CHAPTER 22

It was the policewoman Mrs Woods had called Jill Chambers who answered the door when I rang the lower bell of the house near Brondesbury Park. She stood with the chain holding the door ajar, her WPC's uniform buttons glinting in the shade of the hall, looking at me steadily with that same hint of suspicion that I'd noticed before.

'Mr Simpson. Good morning.'

'Good morning, WPC Chambers. May I come in?'

For a moment she seemed to hesitate. Then she closed the door and I heard the chain being released. When the door swung open again I saw Mrs Woods standing in the living-room doorway with young Jeff peering out from behind her.

'Hello, Mr Simpson.'

'Hello, Tim!'

''Morning, Mrs Woods. Hi, Jeff. It's a clear day and I wondered if I could take Jeff fishing?'

She smiled at me. Her manner had changed. She looked less crushed and more expectant, like anyone who has something to hope for. The WPC pursed her lips, watching me closely.

'Of course.' Mrs Woods looked at the WPC. 'If it's all right?'

She hesitated, looking dubious.

'A precedent has been established,' I said, reasonably and pleasantly. 'I do hope there's no problem with another trip?'

'I'm not sure. We had a little problem yesterday.'

'Oh?'

WPC Chambers flashed a quick, reproachful glance at

Mrs Woods. 'There was quite a panic. Mrs Woods went off —shopping, she says—without letting us know where she'd gone. Got both me and a police officer into trouble.' She gave me a long, searching look. 'She won't say why it took so long. It's been very difficult. We wouldn't like it to happen again.'

'Oh dear.' I kept my expression neutral. 'I hope that won't affect young Jeff coming out for a little fishing trip up at the reservoir? As we did before? You'll know where we will be, won't you?'

'I'll have to check.' She wasn't a bad sort as policewomen go and I felt quite sorry for her, being in that position. 'I'll have to check.'

'All right. I'll wait, shall I?'

She stared at me a bit more and then went out of the front door to gesticulate at a car across the road. Turning half to watch us and half to see her way, she went to the car window and started talking to a plain clothes man inside. I winked at Mrs Woods and put a surreptitious thumb up for her to see.

'They think it's OK,' I whispered. 'I'll get a specialist to check it, but there's a fair chance that it's a real Monet. Could be worth a lot. Keep your fingers crossed.'

She bit her lip in excitement, shivered, and pressed Jeff to her. He gazed at us both uncomprehendingly, so she put her finger to her lips.

'It's a secret, Jeff,' she whispered. 'Good news. Tim'll tell you when you go fishing. But not a word now.'

The policewoman came back up the front path to stand in the doorway. 'They say it will be all right.' She stared at me. 'Inspector Johnson sent you a message. Be sure to keep him posted, he said.'

'I hear you. Can we go?'

'You're to have discreet company. An officer will follow you, just in case.' She gave Mrs Woods another reproachful glance. 'Until this matter is resolved, we need to look after you.'

There was a good deal of bustle them, with Jeff dodging about with his fishing tackle and Mrs Woods getting me a flask of tea and some lemonade for Jeff. The house suddenly became active and excited. Even the policewoman cheered up and chivvied Jeff to get along before the weather turned, now that he had the chance of getting out.

He bubbled with suppressed excitement in the car, in which I told him that the secret would have to wait until we got to the reservoir. It was relatively quiet that morning, even though it was fine, and there were very few anglers dotted about the bank. As before, the air was like a sound muffler, full of dull thuds and the humming of distant traffic. Jeff disposed himself seriously on the concrete edge, setting out his tin of gentles, his rod and reels, a canvas bag of assorted equipment, tins, and a record book for his catches. When it was all set up I put on an anorak and got out a car rug to sit next to him, watching his small excited face under his mousy brown hair and noticing that his thin body was clad in jeans that were very clean, like his thick Tottenham Hotspur windcheater. Mrs Woods obviously doted on Jeff.

'What's the secret?' he demanded. 'Come on, you promised to tell me once we got here.'

I grinned at him and ruffled his hair. 'Can you keep it?'

''Course I can!'

'Can you give one back in exchange?'

He sank his chin into his lapels and pulled a face. 'Maybe.'

'Maybe? Maybe? That's not a promise.'

'I haven't got any secrets,' he protested.

'Ah, now. How do I know that?' I grinned at him, still. 'Never mind, though; I'll tell you. Your mother's got a painting, one your dad had, that might be worth a lot of money. So that's our secret. You mustn't tell anyone because if they find out she might lose it, but we're keeping it safe for her. Don't tell a soul.'

His eyes widened. 'A lot of money? Is it worth a lot of money?'

'Possibly. If it's genuine.'

'How much?'

'Ah. We don't know yet, but quite a lot. An expert has to look at it, to make sure. But we think it's good news.'

'Is it one of my dad's?' He stared at me anxiously.

159

'It belonged to him, yes.'

'No, I mean did he paint it?'

'Oh no. He bought it. It was painted by a man called Monet. A Frenchman.'

'You mean Claude Monet?'

I stared at his seven-year-old face in surprise. 'Yes. Why? How did you know about Claude Monet?'

He grinned knowingly. 'My dad told me all about them French painters. He used to tell me about them while I was fishing. All their life stories and that. Like that one that cut his ear off. Van Goff, I remember him.'

'I bet you remember that one, sure. Gory stuff. What else did he used to tell you about? Sherlock Holmes?'

'Yeah!' The boy's head came up and now it was his turn to look surprised. 'How did you know? He was great on Sherlock Holmes. He used to tell me all about him, an' the hound of the Bas—wait, I'll get it right—Baskervilles, that one, I got it right this time. Me mum said he'd give me nightmares but I never did. How did you know?'

'Just a guess, Jeff.'

'But—but how? Why did you guess?'

I smiled at him and feigned a cunning expression. 'Elementary, my dear Watson. 'Cos I'm a detective too, you see. I've got a hooked pipe and a deerstalker at home.'

'Go on! You're not! You haven't!'

I chuckled and ruffled his hair. 'No, I'm not. And I haven't, but I do have a pal who used to be very keen on Sherlock Holmes and he's a detective, now, a real one, in the police at Scotland Yard.'

'Ahh. I don't like them! Sherlock was a *private* detective. He made the police look silly. He was much cleverer than them.'

I ruffled his hair again. 'Maybe. Maybe not. What else did your dad tell you about? Other artists, too?'

He shrugged. 'Lots of them.' His eye went out to his sinker, which had bobbed just once, misleadingly. 'He knew all about them. I thought you were talking about one of my dad's own paintings, one he did himself, not some boring old French one.'

160

I frowned at him. 'Your father was a restorer, Jeff. He restored other people's paintings. I didn't think he painted much himself.'

'Oh yes he did! He used to show me them, when we were up here fishing. He said it could be our secret. There, now I've told you one back, like you asked.'

'Show you them? Paintings? Here, up at the reservoir?'

'Nah.' He gave me a derisive laugh, grinning at my mock-simplicity. 'Not the actual paintings. Not them. The photographs. The photographs of them.'

'Photographs? What photographs?'

'Of the paintings, silly. The photographs of the paintings. Nice big ones. He liked to think about what happened to them, after. He always had a photograph of them.'

I stared at him. 'I've never seen one, Jeff. No one found anything like that at the studio. No photographs. No one told me of any.'

He grined slyly. 'Can you keep a secret?'

''Course I can!'

'Cross your heart and promise to die.'

'Cross my heart and promise to die.' Over the other side of the reservoir I saw a man in a dark blue anorak walk casually up behind an angler and stare disinterestedly at his kit. One of Sam Johnson's men, I thought, keeping us in sight. Maybe.

'Don't look.' Jeff Woods was rummaging in his fishing bag. 'You're not to look.'

'Why not?' I stared at his bag in his hands as he dug into it.

'It's me diary.' The boy produced an octavo-sized black book. 'I keep all my fishing records in it. And other things.' He grinned sheepishly. 'I'm not showing you those.'

'All right. I won't look. What are you going to show me?' The man in the blue anorak was keeping his distance, which was all right. If anyone had wanted to get Jeff or me or both of us, now was the time when they could do it. If they assumed that Jeff or I, or both of us, had something they wanted. Which was something I still didn't know.

'Here.' He produced a piece of folded card from his black

diary. It was white card, much thumbed and, as he handed it to me, I could see that it was photographic paper.

I took it in my hand. The card was the size of his diary but I now saw that it had been folded into four so that it became small enough to conceal within the octavo covers. Opened up, it would be much bigger, with a cross of creases scored into it.

'That was me dad's last one.' Jeff Woods stared at me, suddenly intense and serious at this sharing of a deep secret. 'I kept it, see? He gave it to me to look at and I hid it in me diary. It was my secret. He never let me keep them. Said he needed them for his files.' Tears were filling his eyes. 'I kept it. I wanted one. He never used to let me.'

I put my arm round his shoulder for a moment. A small boy with his secret. A small boy with something of his dad's to be proud of. Something he would show to no one except those he trusted totally, those who would not mock or deride or say something that would bring shame or embarrassment or humiliation. I opened the card up, carefully turning it over at each crease.

The photograph on the glossy side was of a painting, mainly of a house by a road with a tree at one side and a pair of women walking sedately along. They were wearing Victorian dress. A pair of gates fronted a short driveway leading to a Victorian English house which had a lawn at one side and was typical of those large suburban family houses that the prosperous bourgeoisie could then afford. Behind it, vaguely, was a similar house next door, so that they looked like a pair. The style of the painting was Impressionistic.

The signature at the bottom of the painting was much clearer than that of the Monet. It stared at me in just the same way, though:

C. Pissarro, 1871.

CHAPTER 23

The Impressionists have provided enough stimulus for several bulk tankerloads of verbiage to be written about them. Not to mention the Post-Impressionists and all the other, subsequent developers of imagery and artistic themes. It really is amazing how such visual material can stimulate so much writing, not just about technique and taste, biographical reminiscence and factional argument, but also about politics and economics and social history. All from a chap just painting a painting. The entire structure of major societies, their morals, their military power and their development or decline can, it seems, be analysed from the way in which a painter might daub a bloke and his wife reclining in their favourite sitting-room or standing out in the garden, pruning the roses.

When I had goaded Jeremy with Wilenski's judgement on Monet and Pissarro and Sisley, I may have had some unconscious thought about this in my head. The buying public have very little patience for the judgement of art critics; the values they pay follow other lines of influence. When I mention the buying public, of course it is not a very large public that can afford a million or more for painting but the Japanese, for instance, have just paid forty million dollars for a van Gogh. Wilenski said that van Gogh was a minor artist. So Jeremy was probably right when he advised me to forget Wilenski. Of course it could be argued that it is the tragic story of van Gogh rather than his merits as a painter which has shot him to the top of the price tree, in much the same way as that of Gwen John has made her prices exceed other, technically better painters, including her rakish brother Augustus whose biography was on poor old Mitch Woods's chest in his studio.

I thought about all this as I sat alone in the flat in Onslow Gardens after leaving Jeff Woods at his home. Notice how, without thinking, I said 'the' flat instead of 'my' flat. It had always been my flat, before Sue came to it, but I had got into the habit of thinking of it as 'our' flat as time had passed. Now it was just 'the' flat, a sort of neutral colour, so to speak, occupied by me but not lived in, in any domestic sense. My paintings were still on the walls, my books were still in the bookcase. So were Sue's, awaiting her removal of them. Territory was still occupied, tenuously, by these artefects, which staked an emotional claim to the ground which Kate Theaker had now briefly crossed in perhaps a symbolic way, her presence and her passions rendering the space more public, less personal, open to change, to new directions.

Reading about art was beginning to affect my thinking process. To hell with symbolism, I thought, you've had a blazing row with Sue, one that is going to take a major initiative to repair. You've consoled yourself with a nurse who is using you in a strategic game of marriage negotiations with Redman. Pleasant though it may have been, that is all it is, or was. Better forget that.

I poured myself another whisky. Outside the flat the weather had turned slightly warmer, bringing a nasty, cold, dripping sort of night to the city. Traffic motored about, making more noise than usual. By the kerb under the trees, in a parked car, I knew that a man posted by Sam Johnson was watching me. It was unlikely that they'd actually tapped my phone, but they might have. No doubt the efficient WPC Chambers had reported my second session with Jeff Woods to all her superiors. In my hands, in one way, was the future of Jeff and his mother. In my mind, somewhere, was the solution to all those horrible deaths, the reason for them. If you believed in auto-suggestion, you might never sleep again. It was I who had come straight from Nobby's bedside to that meeting at the Bank. It was I who had suggested, then and there, that we search for a Monet and a Pissarro of London scenes. Now there was a possible Monet in the Bank vaults, a photo of a Pissarro in my jacket and five people dead, murdered.

On the table in front of me was a pile of books on the Impressionists. I knew, now, about the effect of the

Franco-Prussian War and the Paris Commune of 1871 in detail. I knew about the fate of Whistler's pal Courbet and the toppling of the Vendôme column. I was fed up to the teeth with the whole bloody thing.

Next to the pile of books was a neat file, delivered by the Bank's courier from our market research department, with Jeremy's compliments. I had read the whole of the contents carefully. Possibilities flickered about my mind. It was going to be a long night, one without sleep. Black coffee was called for if the whisky was to be prevented from muddling my thoughts. I got up and made some, bringing it back to my desk. In flats like this all over London, single people like me were disposing themselves to spin the night away.

On the table next to the Bank's file was the book the courier had also brought, borrowed from the London Library. I picked it up thoughtfully: *Conan Doyle*, by Hesketh Pearson.

It was going to be a long night. I opened the first page carefully and began to read about the remarkable life of the Irish Scottish Englishman who created the most famous detective in the world.

CHAPTER 24

Tennison Road is now a wide suburban street that humps itself over the multiple railway lines south of Norwood Junction. Most of the houses in it are typically British semi-detached ones from the ribbon development of the pre- and post-war periods, places where commuting Pooters have happily built over the sweet uneventful countryside. The new estate of Lynton Gardens, a cul-de-sac almost opposite the place I parked, is modern and looks as though someone has recently developed the area backing on to school playing fields where team games have not yet been banned as stimulating dangerously competitive feelings in our youth. It struck me as a traditional area, residential, utterly calm in its autumnal mantle of grey London weather. I got out of the car and sniffed the smell of wet leaves in the sharp air. It was very damp. Somewhere over the house-clad hill behind me was the tall pylon of the Crystal Palace transmitter, a high spike I'd glimpsed from various angles on my way to my destination. Turning back from that direction now, to look eastwards to my right, down the street, I saw two large old houses tightly side by side, rearing like sandcastles surrounded by a wash of lower tidal development. With a sense of relief I pulled young Jeff Woods's folded photograph of his father's painting from my pocket and opened it up. It showed the first house, No. 12, quite clearly in the middle ground, whereas the one behind it was more vague and yes, impressionistic. No other houses clogged the painting; the rest of the painted scene was rural and Victorian like most of the Pissarro Norwoods of 1871. With a heart that was starting to thud I crossed the street and stood on the pavement in front of No. 12 to scan the circular blue plaque on the wall, fairly high up to the right.

The plaque was quite simple. It said:

In this house
lived
Sir Arthur Conan Doyle
creator of Sherlock Holmes
1891–1894

and I knew then that the whole ridiculous and tragic story that had started by Nobby's bedside at the hospital was now quite clear to me even though I had nothing to prove it with, nothing but hunch and speculation and theory.

I was still standing staring at the plaque and thinking about it when a red Ford Sierra pulled up behind my car and Sam Johnson got out. He stared across the road at me and then got out to step carefully, as though the tarmacadam might have land-mines within it. He had gone back to wearing his awful brown tie again and I couldn't help wincing once more at the way it clashed with his dark grey suit.

'Hello, Sam,' I said. 'Tell me: was that tie a present or something?'

He scowled. 'Birthday. My mother-in-law. And don't be personal. You look as though you've slept in your clothes.'

'I have. Or rather I haven't. I've been in them all night, anyway. You've managed to shake off Warren for a bit, have you?'

He gave me a straight look. 'Warren only comes for the bodies,' he said. 'Your assurance on the phone that this was to be an explanatory chat and there would be no corpses about has kept him away on much more important topics. Actually, he said that he hadn't got time to be bored by one of your expositions on fine art and detection. Not again. I'm more tolerant, he said, so I had better go alone. So here I am.'

'Bloody cheek. What does he mean, again? I've never given him the real treatment, Sam, never. Not Warren.'

He didn't answer. He was studying the façade of the house and the blue plaque, his eyes focused upwards, his lips moving slightly as he read the inscription. Then his head moved downwards and he turned to me, suspiciously.

'Conan Doyle? Sherlock Holmes? Some sort of joke, is this?'

'Sort of,' I said, handing him the photograph. 'Sort of. A joke that went rather sour and killed a few people, you might say.'

He stared at the photograph for a while. 'That's this house,' he said, eventually. 'Definitely this house. C. Pissarro, 1871? I'm not an Art Squad man but I've heard about Pissarro. Did he paint this?'

'No. I don't think so. In fact I guess this house might not even have been here in 1871. It's timbered a bit in what is usually a slightly later style. But that's not important. Mitch Woods painted this painting. That's what's important.'

'Mitch Woods? How do you know?'

'His son Jeff let me have this yesterday. It was his father's last piece of painting. Jeff pinched one of the copies of the photographs of it and folded it away in his fishing diary. He wanted one of his father's paintings to keep. It was his secret, kept even from his mother. Mitch used to talk to him about painting when they went fishing together, but he never let the boy keep photos of his paintings; they were too hot to risk. Anyway, Mitch used to tell him Sherlock Holmes stories while they were sitting there.'

'Eh?' Sam Johnson flashed a glance up at the blue plaque. 'Sherlock Holmes stories?'

'Yes. It was the odd book out, d'you see? In Mitch's studio, among all those art reference books. Hesketh Pearson's life of Doyle. I borrowed a copy and read it last night. Pearson gives this address; Doyle moved here from Devonshire Place when he started to write the Sherlock Holmes stories and gave up doctoring to be an author. Guess who else is a Sherlock Holmes fan, or used to be?'

He didn't even look at me. His eyes were still on the plaque. 'Nobby Roberts,' he said.

'Correct. When we were at college together he gave a talk to a literary group on Doyle's sources and the fallacies in some of the plots. He wasn't thinking of going into the police, then. But he did, eventually. I know Nobby has always had a strong moral purpose but I've often wondered if Doyle had something to do with his recruitment to the Force. He was dead keen on Holmes.'

'And he's lived on the edge of Dulwich for years.'

'Correct. That's what threw me for a long time. Pissarro painted Dulwich College, you know. I thought that maybe this whole thing was to do with Dulwich, but it wasn't. It was all to do with Norwood. They took Nobby to Dulwich because it was the nearest hospital and it was near his home. But I think he came round here to check up on this painting. And was attacked on his way home.'

'The A213,' Sam said. 'The Selhurst Road. Of course. It crosses the end of this road.'

'Exactly. So there's a connection. And a connection with Mitch Woods. You follow me?'

'There's more than a connection. Forensic confirmed it yesterday. The gun that shot Nobby shot all the others as well. Woods, Goldsworth and the reliner's lot. So the

168

suspicions Nobby had, whatever they were, all tied up in the end.'

'Ha! Suspicions! You remember our lunch at the pub? You remember my remarks about Nobby's reaction to my voice, even in a coma? That this was all about an art caper that I might get my big nose into? You didn't believe me, did you? What do you think now?'

He smiled slightly, his professional expression relaxing. 'I'm not here to think. I'm here to listen to you, telling me. Then I'll judge what I should think. Fortunately for you, I've heard you before, so I'm willing to listen again. Brandon and Warren would rather lock you away for the duration because they think that your mere presence stimulates homicide.' He glanced instinctively up and down the calm suburban street. 'So let's hear it, at last. What is all this about? This part of it, anyway.'

'Oh, I think that you should be telling me that, but you're so darn close, you lot, that a chap has to work it all out for himself. It's about drugs, isn't it? About drug money, to be precise. The laundering of drug money?'

He stared at me, then nodded very slightly, as though reluctant to do so.

'Good. I'm glad you've decided to let me into your confidence at last. The sort of combination an Art Squad and a Fraud Squad man could provide would be most useful for that kind of thing, wouldn't it?'

'Why an Art Squad man?'

'Oh, Sam! Come on. You know as well as I do that art and drugs have been closely associated in many ways. Art stolen to pay for drugs, art bought to launder drug money. But one of the problems of laundering drug money, as everyone knows, is that movements of money on their own raise suspicions in all sorts of ways. What you need are legitimate methods of creating cash flow, of moving money. So just think; supposing you sell paintings, really expensive paintings, to people in places where you want to get your money away from, like say Switzerland? Suppose you don't actually have to buy those paintings? You don't steal them because that creates another crime to hide. You just get a faker to produce a painting, but a painting good enough to fool most experts and then you "sell" it to your accomplice abroad, who sends you the money in London and bingo! you have a nice profitable business in an ideal, exchange-control-free country like England from which you can resend the money to anywhere you like. Or just spend it. Of course you don't sell only fakes. You buy real paintings at auction and you mix the fakes with them in your stock. But you never allow any of the outside public to buy the fakes; they're in your catalogue just to make them legitimate, at astronomic prices, but only for a brief time. They have to exist, of course, physically exist, because auditors and VAT men want physical evidence, stock checks, from time to time, so you have to have actual paintings to show them, but auditors and VAT men aren't art experts, they can't tell a fake from a bag of marbles; they just verify that the item exists.'

Sam frowned. 'You mean you create these—these paint-ings—to satisfy snoopers that they're not just paper records?'

'That's right. You shove the paintings out to your ac-complices in return for the money and no one can say that you didn't make a physical sale, of a physical item with an invoice and transport documents and evidence of despatch of some kind. The joy is that the "buyer" doesn't give a damn whether the painting is kosher or not, in fact he can throw it away once he's got it—if he's so inclined—and he can become hard to trace once the transaction is completed. But you haven't had to take money you can't account for out into the market and buy a Picasso or a Manet or whatever with it and then have people ask awkward ques-tions about where you got the money to buy it from. You just get one of the best fakers, who's a drug addict anyway, to turn out the odd painting for you in return for a fee that keeps him in his addiction. And everyone marvels at how you have a knack of coming up with the odd masterpiece now and again even though you are very expensive and your unknown clients must be crazy. You mustn't do it too often, of course. You have to have a purchase invoice

170

too, probably provided by your faker—or rather "restorer" because quite a lot of restorers deal in paintings as well as restoring them. But you do all that very carefully. It has to be part of an overall plan that launders money, that has about twenty different systems and leads and cross-tracks and all the features that I don't have to tell you about, do I?'

'No,' Sam said. 'You don't. But there could be a problem you haven't dealt with yet.'

'Export licences?'

'Correct. What about export licences?'

'Good point. This is where your element of skill and choice of painting comes in. As long as you don't make the fake paintings too important, not too interesting, you have no problem, because the licensing authorities won't hold the painting up for someone else to make a bid. You get your licence. But if the painting is of national interest you may not, and there could be awkward questions. Nowadays a Pissarro of Norwood would be of great interest. If it was a real one. On the other hand, if a painting was not correctly attributed or was mis-labelled, there'd be no delay. And paintings that are not so terribly valuable but still above the £16,000 level which dictates the need for an export licence wouldn't arouse too much interest, but then you'd only be moving relatively small sums of money. In this case, however, the painting wasn't going abroad, so no export licence was needed.'

'No?'

'No. I think not. I assume that sometimes there is drug money here in this country that needs to be laundered? That just needs cleaning up here? The painting wasn't going abroad this time, it was to launder some UK money. That's why an expensive English subject could be used, an important one even, that involved a lot of money. The problem was that, in this case, Mitch Woods was too clever by half.' I sighed as I looked up again at No. 12 Tennison Road, Norwood. 'Morris Goldsworth said that Mitch was brilliant. His fakes were very good. But Mitch did it for the joy of fooling experts as much as for the money. He used to build in a spot-the-deliberate-mistake into his paintings sometimes. This time he was too clever by half.' I gestured at the house. 'He painted number twelve here. It was his little joke. After all, it was a genuine Norwood house and it was old. He never suspected that anyone serious would look at the painting or, indeed, the photographs of it. Not in detail. But there, sauntering down Bond Street, checking up on an idea he had had, came Nobby Roberts. First he dropped in for a chat with Morris Goldsworth. Then he went on his merry way. And blow me if, for good reasons of his own, Nobby didn't go into Kennard & Crowe and look casually through their catalogue. The timing was extraordinary because it can't have been in the catalogue long, the painting that stopped him in his tracks. Morris certainly didn't know about this painting because I was waiting all along for him to mention it or to try and locate it, to try and sell it to me, but he didn't. He never knew about it. Anyway, Nobby saw the photograph and that led him to spot the tomfoolery.'

Sam scratched his chin dubiously. 'You mean he knew? He knew this house, just like that? From the painting?'

'I don't know. Not immediately, probably not. I don't think he did. I think he had a vague flash of memory. After all, he lives not all that far away and he was always a keen Holmes fan. Something probably made him stiffen and frown and wonder when he saw the catalogue. Something that made him dig into his memory and something that gave his suspicions away to Kennard & Crowe. You see, a few days ago I bought a sort of brochure-book on Pissarro's work here. *Camille Pissarro at the Crystal Palace* by Nicholas Reed. It shows all the known paintings he did here—I even looked at two of them in the National Gallery—and it charts every single one of them. Twelve oil paintings and some sketches. What's more, this book sorts out where they were painted and what of, from what angle. Pissarro went back to France in 1871 and finished off a lot of them there using the sketches he'd made during his stay. He mis-titled them from lack of memory. *Church on Westow Hill in Snow* isn't on Westow Hill at all; it's All Saints, Beulah Hill. *Penge Station,*

Upper Norwood isn't that either; it's the old Lordship Lane station. And so on. This guy and one called Martin Reid have researched the whole thing. There's a map and a list of all the paintings and sketches and a list of where they all are now, in London and America and Europe. Only one is missing: a winter scene. It is conceivable that there might be others though, these things do happen, odd unexpected paintings do turn up, by famous artists, that have never been catalogued or provenanced. Ask any dealer. So one has to keep an open mind, even if one's name is Nobby Roberts and you know all these things and you've got a copy of that same book yourself at home.

'But Nobby has something of my own brand of curiosity. He decided to check on that painting for himself. I assume he was following up the laundering of drug money. You said at Kilburn that he was looking into financial aspects. Some lead or another led him to Kennard & Crowe. I've checked on them myself via the Bank's research department. They're all UK resident directors but the business is owned by a group which in turn has a major Cayman Island shareholding, which in turn is owned by a Bahamas set-up. The Bahamas is a known drug-trading centre, yes?'

'Yes.' Sam nodded briskly now. 'Nobby Roberts had a series of Bahamas and Cayman Islands and other tax haven leads to follow. But there were hundreds of them. Weeks of work.'

'Nobby was on the Art Fraud Squad, remember? All sorts of old associations could have sparked him off. But he went into Kennard & Crowe's for a snoop, looked through their catalogue and decided that the Pissarro wasn't what it should be, or something, and came to have a look. That's my theory. And something he said or did made them follow him. They probably nearly had a heart attack when they saw what the painting Mitch Woods had supplied them portrayed: Conan Doyle's house in Norwood. Nobby probably burst out laughing once his doubts were confirmed. But they knew he'd never let go of a fake trail like that, even if it had nothing to do with drugs. It was so blatant to Nobby. How to cock a snook at the art trade, by Mitch

173

Woods. You art experts are so clever: real detectives, you are. See if you can spot this one. Genuine Lower Norwood scene, ungenuine Pissarro. Of the house where Sherlock Holmes stories were being written? Hogwash.'

'Woods must have been crazy.' Sam Johnson spoke wonderingly. 'Mad. Totally cracked. Cocaine must have affected his brain.'

'Not really. Not cocaine, anyway. Money, perhaps. Mitch Woods was over the top actually, I agree. Bomb-happy. In the clouds. Trying to suppress his joy until he could get clear. I reckon he intended this to be his last painting for the drugs mob. He was getting out. He was quietly thumbing his nose at the world. I think he was aiming to scarper, do a bunk, disappear. Mitch Woods had come into a fortune and no one knew but him.'

'A fortune? What fortune?'

I leant against the gatepost. 'After years of faking and scraping, Mitch actually bought, fair and square, buried in a lot on a market stall, a genuine Monet. For peanuts.'

'What? A Monet? How do you know?'

'Because I've got it, safely locked up in the vaults at the Bank.' I didn't look at him. 'His widow brought it to me the other day. It was in with a lot of prints and watercolours and a painting of a horse. I'm willing to bet that he didn't paint it and I shall have it authenticated soon. Then I'll buy it for our Art Fund. I very much doubt if the valuation will be under a million.'

Sam Johnson opened his mouth and focused burning eyes on me. I held up a defensive hand. 'Before you say anything rash, let me give you my excuse. I promised my client confidentiality and until last night I wasn't sure if it was genuine. And actually the Monet doesn't have anything to do with Nobby and the reliners or Morris Goldsworth. That was all to do with the Pissarro. Once they knew that Nobby suspected the Pissarro, they had to eliminate all trace of it, otherwise the game was blown. Nobby would be on to tracing the purchaser, sources of funds, as well as of the painting. They must have followed him here. Once he'd looked at Doyle's house and they realized the joke, they knew he'd be suspicious. So they tried to eliminate him. Then they shot Mitch Woods, partly as a punishment and partly to make sure that no one would trace anything back to him. Of any sort. There was no work in progress in Mitch's studio, which was odd; they must have removed it. Then I guess they must have seen Morris Goldsworth at Mitch's studio within minutes of the murder and Morris was a known expert on Pissarro and Norwood. The dreadful irony is that I believe that Mitch wanted to talk to Morris about how to handle the Monet, nothing to do with the Pissarro. But they got the wrong impression, you might say. These people are absolutely ruthless. They knew Mitch's methods and I suspect that the Pissarro was relined. The reliner always photographed his client's work so they had to fix him too, after they made sure that he'd told them of everything he might have.'

I stopped. The memory of the reliner's and what they had done made me pause. Sam said nothing. 'That's my theory, as I've said.' I waved the photograph at him. 'By the time I visited Kennard & Crowe they'd whipped their copy of the photo out of their catalogue; it probably wasn't intended to be in there for long and it was bad luck again that I happened to see it mentioned in the index, which was still unaltered. All other traces had gone. It was mischievous of Mitch to use this house for his fake but he never thought a sleuth would follow it up. The painting wasn't supposed to go on to the genuine market. Poor old Mitch was over the top, within sight of wealth at last, genuine wealth for once, not from fakery. Bitter, isn't it? Bloody bitter, I'd say.'

There was a silence. Sam Johnson went back to staring unbelievingly at the blue plaque, as though willing it to tell him something.

'It fits,' he said, eventually. 'It all fits. It means that our work is just starting, though. We'll have to do a complete job on Kennard & Crowe. A full audit of all transactions and purchasers. It'll be a dawn raid. The problem is that they'll have had time to clean the place out already, because of what's happened.' He looked at me curiously. 'I wonder why they haven't had a go at you?'

175

'Thanks very much! I suppose because they think I haven't seen anything or got any concrete evidence. They must have cleared any photos from Mitch Woods's studio when they murdered him and they obviously didn't know about this extra print. And you lot have been hanging round Mrs Woods and Jeff so they've kept clear of them up to now.'

'It's a good job they didn't know she escaped to see you,' Sam Johnson said reprovingly. 'She might have known something incriminating.'

'She didn't, though. Mitch never told her what he was doing, never.'

'They might not have banked on that.'

I shrugged. From the railway line down the road came the sound of an electric train rushing by. When Pissarro had painted in the region and Conan Doyle wrote his books, it had all been steam. In their real existence they had missed each other by twenty years, but now a dead faker of paintings had connected them. I shook my head.

'I'd better borrow that.' Sam held his hand out for the photograph. 'Don't worry, you'll get it back.'

'I promised Jeff Woods.'

He hesitated. 'If he knew what it had done to his father, he might not want it.'

'So no one will tell him.'

'No.' He folded the photo carefully away into his pocket as we walked back to our cars. 'We've a lot to do. But we'll be in touch.' He bit his lip and stared at me for a moment, looking as though he was going to say something, but he didn't. Then he got into the Ford Sierra and wound down the driver's window. I stood next to his car for a moment.

'Tell me something, Sam.'

'What?'

'Am I allowed to see Nobby now?'

He smiled. 'I should think so. Subject to that doctor's approval. I'll arrange for you to be cleared from our side, but wait until tomorrow; he's having a visit from Brandon today. They're hoping there's a chance he'll be fit enough

176

to talk for a few minutes. Nothing comprehensive; just a minute or two.'

'Good news?'

'Possibly good news. It'll be interesting to hear, if he has few of the normal amnesia characteristics, whether what he can say fits your theory. We'll be in touch, Tim. Don't emigrate, will you?'

'Oh no,' I said. 'I won't emigrate.'

He backed his car out from behind mine and shot off with a squeal of tyres. I watched him disappear down the street and then sat down behind the wheel of the Jaguar, feeling suddenly very tired and deflated. The house opposite looked down on me, reminding me that Doyle left it because his wife got tuberculosis and they had to go to Switzerland. That led me to thinking about sanatoriums and sanatoriums led to hospitals and how I would be able to go and see Nobby, soon. There he would be, swathed in bandages, but getting better. That cheered me up for a moment.

Only for a moment, though.

Nobby was getting better; the only thing connecting Kennard & Crowe with the fake Pissarro and Mitch Woods, now, was Nobby. Jeff could swear it was painted by his father but only Nobby could swear in court that that painting had been in Kennard & Crowe's catalogue, available for sale. To trace anyone else who could swear to it was virtually impossible. Nobby was the only one who could make any kind of case hang together. Without Nobby the whole thing could be pure speculation and Nobby was due to come round at any moment now and possibly start spilling the beans.

If I were in their shoes, as ruthless as them, I knew what I'd do.

I shot away from the kerb at twice the speed of Sam Johnson, heading the Jaguar back for inner London.

CHAPTER 25

The hospital entrance was no different. The same reddish-brown glazed tiles, the same swing doors that didn't settle together. The porter was eating a sandwich, dropping crumbs on to his uniform, and the matron wasn't typing, she was drinking a mug of what smelled like burnt turnip soup. The young policeman was sitting down, leafing through a magazine. It was very calm.

They all looked up as I burst in through the doors. None of them moved.

'My, my,' the young policeman said. 'Look who's back. In a hurry, too. Just in time to cop a swing at Commander Brandon, I suppose?'

'What?'

'Commander Brandon. He's waiting to see Chief Inspector Roberts. With the doctor and the specialists. It's an important day, today. First hopes of questioning him.'

'Now?'

'Yes, now. Well, they'll have to wait a bit, actually. I suppose. Until the specialists have seen him.' The policeman gave me a self-important look, the look of a man in the know. 'Got to clear it with the specialists first, haven't they?'

'Specialists?'

'Sure.'

'What specialists?'

The policeman put on a patient, dealing-with-the-public expression. 'The specialists who have just arrived to see him. We are talking of Chief Inspector Roberts, aren't we? The Commander arrived at the same time and escorted them himself personally.'

The fat matron frowned. 'What specialists?'

The porter brushed crumbs off his uniform. 'From the Middlesex. Arrived while you were getting your soup. Identification cards, they had. Gladstone bags an' all. Proper specialists, they were. Two of them.'

The fat matron bridled indignantly. 'From the Middlesex? The Middlesex? We've never had to have specialists from the Middlesex here. We don't need specialists here. We are a specialist—'

I went past the policeman and down the corridor at a knee-twinging run that would have out-accelerated the best fly-half of my years any time. Sheer terror lent power to my legs.

'Oy!' shouted the young policeman, dropping his magazine and starting after me. 'Come back! You can't pass here!'

I had a good start on him going through the first set of swing doors and down the corridor with the disgusting trolleys all along it, but I half-collided with an aide and trolley which suddenly came out of a side door leading to a ward, so he caught up slightly as I raced the last bit to the door to the ante-room to Nobby's ward. I went in through that door hearing the sound of his great squeaking rubber boots as he sprinted after me.

They were lined up against one wall. Brandon, Redman, the big sergeant called Birtwhistle, and Kate Theaker. They had their hands on their heads. Facing them was an overcoated man with a sawn-off shotgun. A Gladstone bag lay open on the floor. Going through the connecting door to Nobby's room was another overcoated man with an automatic pistol in his hand, raising it as he entered so that my eye naturally went up to see the bandaged figure on the bed beyond as my momentum carried me straight at him.

The double-barrelled shotgun swung round, but not fast enough to traverse on to me because I was going at the man with the automatic pistol like a bull at a gate. I heard a yell and an explosion and then another yell as the young policeman, arriving too late to catch the blast, hit the man from one side while Birtwhistle hit him a donkey-dropper from behind. But by that time I had problems of my own.

I heard the stammer of the automatic pistol going off as the second man turned to face me and I ran into him with one arm up under the chin, maul-fashion. Then we collided and crashed into the room beyond, collapsing in a heap at the foot of Nobby's bed. The automatic scuttered to the skirting.

I rolled off him quickly to get my legs back under me but, in trying to prise myself up, I found my left arm didn't work. I missed my purchase and rolled back somehow, away from him. He got one leg up under himself and jumped for the gun. From the floor I saw him pick it up as I tried to roll back the other way but, maddeningly, I couldn't do it. It was as though my whole side was paralysed. Of course, I suddenly thought, I must have been shot. I could see quite clearly and even think, but the co-ordination had gone and my one arm wouldn't obey any signals while my legs didn't seem to be helping either. With amazing clarity I saw the man raise the gun and turn it to point first at Nobby on the bed. I opened my mouth to shout but only a sort of hoarse catcall came out.

Quite deliberately he raised the gun to get an angle over Nobby's plastercast leg, which obscured his line of fire. As he did it, the burly Sergeant Birtwhistle burst through the doorway and achieved the ambition of a lifetime: he put three police .38 revolver bullets, one after the other, at point blank range, into the gunman, not even stopping after the first two shots, which jerked the man violently away from the edge of the bed and over to the wall where a splash of blood clotted on to the cream paint. Birtwhistle then shot him again, savagely. It was a miracle, in a way, that Birtwhistle was able to stop after his third shot, but then they tell me that police training does induce caution in these matters. Of a sort, anyway.

Birtwhistle turned to look at me and spoke, but I didn't catch what he said. I was diverted by the sight of Nobby's head, which, devoid of most of its bandages, was a distinct patchwork of pale skin, nasty blood scabs and tufts of ginger hair in disparate places. If it hadn't looked painful, it might have been quite comic.

I hadn't felt much up to then, but now I started to get a very nasty, sick, aching sensation spreading through my chest and up my neck, the sort of ugly feeling that you get

180

after a very bad knock playing rugby, one that makes you know, as you are lying there in the mud, that this is going to be a long job and that they will have to carry you away, on a stretcher, off the field.

CHAPTER 26

I was ill for a long time. They told me afterwards that the operation to remove the bullets was very tricky and they had to get a specialist, a real specialist this time, from an army unit in Aldershot, to come and operate. Brandon insisted he was flown in by helicopter. I was unconscious, on and off, for about a week. In nightmares I saw the faces of everybody, particularly Morris Goldsworth, to the extent that I was sure that I'd snuffed it and that this was the ante-room to Purgatory or something. But then one day I felt more conscious and there, ironically, was Brandon, leaning over me with Sam Johnson behind him, peering at me anxiously.

'A medal,' Brandon was saying, 'definitely a medal. No question about it. I shall resign if they don't. Saved the lives of five people. No question. Remarkable timing. Gratitude of the whole Force.'

I didn't want a medal. I felt dreadful and I wanted to know what had happened. It took an effort to get out a hoarse croak.

'Was I right?'

'Right?' Brandon looked puzzled.

'About them. The Pissarro?' I felt too ill and weak to spell it all out.

Brandon's face cleared. 'Oh. Yes. Of course. Yes, you were. Sam here will tell you all about it when you're well enough. Clearing-up operation, reasonable results. The shotgun fellow talked in the end, luckily, because there was nothing by way of evidence at Kennard & Crowe's. But Roberts confirmed it all. We got some of the network. Confiscated the stock. As much as we could hope for this

181

time. I think you've had enough; we'd better leave you. Take it easy. Plenty of time.'

I noticed they were looking at me strangely, like people looking at a curiosity, but perhaps that was just the effects of the drugs I was being given and the shock. I'd been shot once before, in Brighton, but this felt much worse, much more serious. I was older and I wasn't certain I'd ever come right again. Or even live.

At some point between two bouts of oblivion I came round, feeling a bit less terrible, and saw Kate Theaker in her uniform sitting beside me, looking at me anxiously. She put a finger to her lips when she saw I was awake.

'Shh,' she said. 'I'm not supposed to be here. I bribed the ward sister; she's an old friend.' She held up her left hand and I saw a ring on the third finger. 'Tony Redman and I are engaged. Thanks to you. Twice over. When the gunmen came in we all thought it was the end. I think that's what finally made Tony's mind up. He'd be very cross if he knew I was here, though. I'm not sure if he'll come and thank you.'

She leant over the bed and kissed me very gently on the cheek, close to the corner of my mouth. I couldn't feel anything, damn it.

'Dear Tim,' she said. 'I'll never forget you, you know. Never.'

Then she stood up. I managed to speak.

'Kate?'

'Yes? What is it?'

'Am I going to be all right?'

Her face went serious. 'Haven't they told you anything?'

'No.'

She looked down at me. 'Can you move your fingers? Gently, now.'

'Yes. I mean no. Not my left ones.'

'That's just your broken arm. That'll mend. What about your toes? Gently, as well.'

I tried. 'Yes, I think so. Yes.'

She slid a hand under the bedclothes and squeezed in a place I won't mention. 'Can you feel that?'

'Cor. You bet.'

She stood up briskly, smoothed the sheet, and grinned down at me in a professional way. 'Then I don't think you've anything to worry about. Not knowing you.'

She kissed me again, once, and was gone.

She was wrong about Redman. He did come and see me, even though I wasn't his case, and he thanked me sincerely enough. Then he said that he had a special visitor for me, one only allowed by special permission, his special permission. He'd allowed it because he was having such trouble with his patient. It was the only way to get any peace and ensure that he could get on with his treatment.

They wheeled Nobby in on a strange sort of wheelchair-cum-stretcher, in which he half reclined, half sat up, still bandaged and plastered but much more recognizably Nobby, with more ginger hair than the last time I'd seen him even though there were traces of scars and cuts on him. They left him propped beside me and he half lay there and glared at me with pinkish eyes.

'You certainly are the most stupid bugger I've ever heard of,' he said.

'Thanks.'

'You can't keep your broken nose out of anything, can you? You are such a burke, you are. Gillian says so, too.'

'Really? Doesn't sound like my Gilly.'

'You're incorrigible. Impossible. I've heard all about it from Sam. You won't be told anything, will you? You're dreadful. You never change.'

'People don't, Nobby. People never change. You should know that.'

He frowned slightly at that, puckering bits of scar tissue on his patchy head. 'How are you? They said you were better but you look pretty terrible to me.'

'You're right. I nearly died, Nobby. Then I thought I was paralysed. There's a lot of damaged pipework within, so to speak. It's going to be a long job, this.'

'Me too.' He grinned suddenly. 'A least I've got the option. Thanks to you.'

'My pleasure. I owed you one, I seem to recall. From Brighton.'

'I forgot that long ago. And you should have, too.' He stared at me reproachfully and I knew that he was referring to the opposite sex, but he wasn't going to raise the subject then, good fellow that he is. He might have known something that I didn't, via Gillian, but it wasn't the time to talk about that.

'I'll be seeing you at physiotherapy eventually,' he said, with the energetic realism so characteristic of him. 'They never leave you in peace in a hospital, you know.'

'I know. Just tell me one thing: did you know that was Doyle's house? When you saw the photo of the Pissarro in Kennard & Crowe's catalogue?'

'Oh yes, of course. I visited that house long ago. Doyle used to practise golf shots on the lawn at the side. The lawn's built over now, although the present owner has a putting green at the back. I must admit that only real fans ever bother about the place; Doyle's best-known house was a place called Undershaw, at Hindhead in Surrey. Not many people know of the Norwood connection; it's a bit like Raymond Chandler—the Philip Marlowe author—he was in Norwood as a boy and went to Dulwich, you know.'

'Yes. I know.'

'Don't sound so bored. My face must have been a picture when I saw the catalogue. Very bad of me; gave the game away.'

'Bit of a shock for you, though. No wonder you reacted.'

'Yes. I couldn't help it. Mind you, I wasn't expecting to be slaughtered as a result. They tell me, by the way, that I reacted when you came to see me, too.'

'You did, Nobby.'

'I'm going to have to work on that.' He paused. 'Tim? You've gone a sort of green colour, like the paint in the corridor. I'd better ring for someone. I came here to thank you very much, not to kill you, you old front-row war-horse.'

The next visitor, much later, the first from the outside world, you might say, was Jeremy White. Jeremy is old-fashioned about such things; he may be a City whizz-kid but family and Bank obligations are imperatives to him. His arrival lifted me from a bad bout of nausea and mental gloom.

'See how the Fates their gifts allot,' he fluted, sitting down next to my bed and smiling kindly upon me.

'For A is happy, B is not.'

'Precisely, dear boy, precisely. You and I have both been Gilbertians from the start. I often reflect that there is something distinctly Savoyard about the whole area of merchant banking these days.'

'You are A, I take it? The happy one?'

'Indeed I am. The acquisition of the Monet—of the Pool of London, no less—will be a major coup for the Art Fund. A really major coup, silencing those board idiots for some time. I cannot congratulate you enough, really I can't. It is quite the most spectacular acquisition to date. A Whistler of Wapping and a Monet of the Pool of London, in the same collection! We are becoming a force, dear boy, a palpable force. I've always said that the Impressionists—no, I'd better not, had I, not with you looking like that.'

'Bad, is it?'

His manner changed. He leant forward anxiously and peered at me, his blond hair reflecting the light on the bedhead next to the saline drip. 'How are you, dear boy? I mean, we've all been dreadfully worried about you. All of us. Mary very much so. And Sue, you know, she—' he broke off for a second—'well, she'll tell you herself. Soon. But how are you? How do you feel?'

'I've known better days, Jeremy.'

'You saved their lives! They say so! The amazing thing is that this time you had the whole thing buttoned up without any danger to yourself, Sam Johnson says, and then, right at the end—dear old Nobby Roberts would have come to a sticky finish, they say, without you.'

'Sergeant Birtwhistle is the one, not me.'

'You're too modest, dear boy. Always have been. Much too modest. I want you to understand that.' He sat back a bit and scratched his jaw. 'I must say, though, that it hasn't done you any good.' The anxious look remained. 'I say,

185

Tim, have the quacks chatted to you at all? I mean, you are going to be all right, aren't you? I couldn't understand a word of what they told me.'

I thought of Sister Kate Theaker for a moment and smiled a smile he didn't understand. 'I'll get better, Jeremy, don't worry. It'll take a bit of time, though.'

'All the time you need! Tim, dear boy, take all the time you need. I feel personally responsible, you know.'

'You? Why?'

'Because of the Art Fund. These things always seem to crop up. What are we going to do? More important, what are you going to do?'

'Me? Do?'

'Tim, dear boy, you can't go on like this.' He became embarrassingly serious. 'Really you can't. Life isn't a game of rugger, you know, in which you can go on taking the risk of getting knocks like this. It's appalling! God knows what will happen the next time. I've started to think, you know, that you really do need someone to look after you, someone who can persuade you to stop dashing out and getting yourself killed. I suppose, er, I suppose—'

His eye caught mine, and he stopped. I had a momentary flash from, oddly enough, Hesketh Pearson. He described Doyle as a writer for boys who were half-men and men who were half-boys. Men who were half-boys; that had described me all right. Did he but know it, it had described Jeremy too. Not that we hadn't grown up a good deal in the last four or five years, we had, but we hadn't quite got there, yet. Jeremy was much nearer, with his wife Mary and the two children, but I was still a lad at heart, trying to avoid life's realities, like most people I know. I understood what Jeremy meant; he didn't have to go further.

He harrumphed and looked at the floor. 'I thought we might set up a trust fund for Mrs Woods and the boy,' he said. 'With the money from the painting, I mean. Woman like that will need a lot of professional advice. Independent advice, with her and the boy's interests at heart. Who better than us?'

'Good idea.'

'I wondered if you might like to be one of the Trustees? Give you a chance to keep an eye on the boy, perhaps? If you agree?'

'I'd be delighted. Tell him—Jeff, I mean—tell him I'll take him fishing as soon as I can. Once I'm half better.'

'Of course. You're looking washed out; I'd better go. I'll come back soon. Bring some champagne. We'll celebrate.'

'That will be nice.'

'Tim, you will think about things a bit, won't you, please? I mean, we've got lots to do at the Bank and we'll still have plenty of fun but I get very worried about you and Mary's absolutely berserk about you and, well, you know who I mean—I say, Tim? Good God, he's gone to sleep.'

I had heard the last words but I was sliding back into unconsciousness by then, slowly descending into a warm, comfortable abyss that, for the first time, didn't threaten to be permanent. I felt safe in it, knowing that I would surface again soon and that the faces that appeared to me were not now bidding me farewell but were waiting, circling me, watching me return.

When I came to the surface again it was bright daylight and a nurse was tidying me up.

'That's better,' she said. 'You can have some tea today. Your visitor might like some, too.'

She disappeared and I lay staring at the closed door. My left arm was still useless beside me but the right one worked quite well. I gave my toes a vigorous twirl.

'Not bad,' I said, out loud.

The door opened and Sue came in, alone, smartly dressed but hesitant at the door, looking at me cautiously before entering and closing it carefully behind her.

'Hello, Sue,' I said, trying to keep calm.

She walked to the side of the bed and sat down on the chair there, her eyes large in her face.

'You look awful,' she said. 'I had no idea—well—I imagined—but I can see, now.'

'Oh? Actually, I've been much worse. Today I'm rather well.'

187

'I've waited this long . . .' she hesitated for a moment. 'I've waited this long because I knew that if I came straight away, while you were nearly dead and they said you could easily die, I wouldn't be able to control myself. I wanted to come later, like this, when things were calmer and clearer and I could be quite sure. Absolutely sure, I mean. Not when I was hysterical or something.'

I didn't understand this, so I waited to see what was to come.

'You're so *stupid*,' she said suddenly, 'so bloody stupid, Tim! You charge off in all directions. You let everyone use you. Everyone. That nurse used you. She's got what she wanted, now. That doctor. Jeremy uses you. The police use you. You let anyone use you when you're off on one of these things. Look at you! You look terrible. You may never be the same again. What are you going to do?'

'Do? I shall get better and go back to work. What else does a man do? I agree I shan't be quite the same again: I shall be much wiser.'

She shook her head and bit her lip. I noticed, now, that she was trembling.

'You use me,' I said gently, seeing the way quite clear. 'You use me like everyone else. The fact that I've liked it doesn't matter. You want your career and you want your freedom but you want me and to be able to tell me what I can do or can't do. We all use each other, but we can't give each other ultimatums in those circumstances, Sue. Not in that way. We can have a lot of freedom and we can have careers but we can't go on as we were.'

She blinked, making the big eyes vanish disconcertingly for a moment. 'We can't?'

'No. We can't.'

She trembled visibly now. 'I was going to say that I love you and I want to come back and I've nearly gone *mad* thinking about you while I kept deliberately away. I've thought about nothing but you.'

'So have I. About you.'

'Well then?' It was a cry. 'You are such a fool, Tim! I try to make you see reason, but you won't.'

I shook my head. 'It can't be, Sue. Unless you marry me, we can't go on as we are.'

'What?'

'I said that unless you marry me the situation is impossible. I'm sorry, but that's how it is. I can't see reason without that.'

She stood up, straight off the chair. Her blue eyes, wide again, flashed at me. 'Are you asking me to marry you? Lying there, looking like that?'

'For the third and last time, yes I am. This is the last time. I mean it. I shan't ask you again.'

'And I have no choice?'

'No,' I said. There, that was what you wanted, wasn't it, I thought, not to be given any choice. An ultimatum really, I suppose.

'You bastard! I thought you were giving me the push! And now what you are saying is that unless I marry you you won't see reason and that it's all over between us?'

'Absolutely. Kaput. Finished.'

She sat back down on the chair. 'In that case,' she said, 'there's no decision to take at all, is there? The answer has to be yes.'

'Yes?'

'Yes!'

And at that point she left the chair and kissed me, not gently or affectionately at all. Very violently, in fact.

It's maddening to be an invalid at a moment like that. But I can tell you, I felt a lot better. In fact, I was quite ready for the champagne which Jeremy burst in with, the cunning devil, three minutes later.